# MYTHICAL CREATURES *of* MAINE

## Fantastic Beasts from Legend and Folklore

CHRISTOPHER PACKARD

Illustrated by Dan Kirchoff

Down East Books

CAMDEN, MAINE

Down East Books
An imprint of Globe Pequot, the trade division of The Rowman & Littlefield Publishing Group, Inc.
4501 Forbes Blvd., Ste. 200
Lanham, MD 20706
www.rowman.com

Distributed by NATIONAL BOOK NETWORK



British Library Cataloguing in Publication Information available

**Library of Congress Cataloging-in-Publication Data**
Names: Packard, Christopher, 1976– author. | Kirchoff, Dan, illustrator.
Title: Mythical creatures of Maine : fantastic beasts from legend and folklore / Christopher Packard ; illustrated by Dan Kirchoff.
Description: Lanham : Derrydale Press, [2021] | Includes bibliographical references. | Summary: "Based on meticulous research into regional legends and folk tales, this volume is an encyclopedia, a field guide to the creatures that can be found in Maine and beyond. While the tales are whimsical and fun, they can also be considered serious scholarship"—Provided by publisher.
Identifiers: LCCN 2021010617 (print) | LCCN 2021010618 (ebook) | ISBN 9781608937264 (cloth) | ISBN 9781608937271 (epub)
Subjects: LCSH: Animals, Mythical—Maine—Ecyclopedias. | Animals—Maine—Folklore—Encyclopedias. | Animals—Mythology—Maine—Ecyclopedias.
Classification: LCC GR825 .P22 2021 (print) | LCC GR825 (ebook) | DDC 398.24/5409741—dc23
LC record available at https://lccn.loc.gov/2021010617
LC ebook record available at https://lccn.loc.gov/2021010618

∞™ The paper used in this publication meets the minimum requirements of American National Standard for Information Sciences—Permanence of Paper for Printed Library Materials, ANSI/NISO Z39.48-1992.

*To my clan of Packards.*
*We each have our stories to tell and we're family.*
*I hope we never forget it.*

# CONTENTS

# ACKNOWLEDGMENTS

**I GRATEFULLY** acknowledge and thank my family, who believed in me and supported my passion for this work. I could not have done this without the support of my wife, children, and parents. I'm also grateful to my cousins and my uncle for sharing with me some of their recollections of these creatures and our family. Thanks specifically to Jerry Packard for the photographs of Burton Marlborough. Special thanks also to my editors at Down East Books and Rowman & Littlefield; without their belief and hard work, this book would certainly not have been possible.

I also appreciate the conversations people shared with me regarding these creatures and French culture. There are certainly too many to name, but I am especially grateful for the communications I shared with Justin Godin, Trish Honaker-Ortiz, Joyce Harrison, and Dr. Walter Jakubas. Not all of them were long, but these all came at just the right moments.

This work would not have been possible without the many librarians who helped me. I appreciate the important work you do as the guides and guardians of our collective knowledge. The work of the nonprofit Native Languages of the Americas and their website (native-languages.org) was also invaluable. Finally, thank you to Lenwood Sharpe and Lumberwoods, Unnatural History Museum for making so many historic resources freely and easily available to the public at lumberwoods.org—these helped get this project off the ground.

Thanks also to all those who pass on the tales of these creatures. And especially to the many people who are no longer with us who took the time to write down some of what they knew so that it would not be forgotten.

# INTRODUCTION

**MAINE IS** well known for its natural beauty. People come from around the world to experience the wildlife, forests, and coastlines of Maine, but few know of its richness in wonderous and magical creatures as well. Many of these mysterious creatures are well known to the Native Americans and have been here for millennia. Some arrived with the French and English settlers, while others were discovered more recently by people who work, play, and live outdoors. While this book is a field guide centered on Maine, the creatures' ranges extend well beyond the state—some even across the country. This guide will also be especially useful to anyone in New Hampshire, Vermont, Massachusetts, New Brunswick, Nova Scotia, Southeast Quebec, and the waters that surround them.

This book is a guide to both truth and story. The creatures described here do not just exist in myth and legend—they really exist if you know how to see them. Throughout human history, our world has always been populated with wondrous creatures; they are there for those with the desire and patience to find them. But today, in our own busy-ness, we usually miss these opportunities and never meet the wondrous beings that share our world. Most of the creatures found in these pages were far more familiar when life was slower and less full of distractions.

Today, it is difficult to imagine a world where people would spend enough time in wilderness to get to know the wondrous things that live there. But imagine Maine in the 1800s. It was a place of unbroken wilderness and no electricity, a place where rivers and railroads were the best highways. In the 1800s, cities had just begun to spring up, and Bangor was one of the richest cities in North America. Maine's wealth was fueled by the resources of the forest and the sea. It was here that the French, British, and Native American Wabanaki peoples lived and shared their stories together. They were all lumbermen, river drivers, guides, trappers, market hunters, sailors, fishermen, and gum pickers who made their living from the land. These were the people who had the time to discover strange creatures and share stories of them with each other around a fire.

But times have changed; our young nation has always been in a hurry to grow up. We move fast, and some of what we had is now lost, like Maine's wolves, mountain lions, and caribou, as well as our mighty American elm and chestnut trees. If we don't take the time to discover and preserve the creatures described in these pages, they will be gone forever. In fact, some may already be lost—beyond recovery.

Many of the fabulous creatures in these pages were best known to lumbermen. When the easy-to-harvest wood was gone, the lumber camps and their stories went west, following Paul Bunyan's trail into new, uncut forests. To each new place lumbermen brought some of the creatures they had already discovered while also finding a new set of unlikely critters. Creatures of the lumberwoods are born of strength and humor. They are known to folklorists as "fearsome critters." In some ways, these critters are a personification of the adversity the lumberjacks faced in the forests they were cutting. Today the critters of the lumberwoods are as endangered as Maine's Atlantic salmon. It is my intention to save them all and to bring them back if I can.

In some of the more remote parts of Maine, these creatures and their stories still flourish. They have been kept alive by the guides and woodsmen whose families have been there since the nineteenth century. They are perhaps less fearsome now and instead funnier and more mysterious, not because the forest has been tamed, but perhaps because our relationship with it is changing. My family is living proof of their survival. I spent my childhood summers chasing sidehill gougers, peltin thumpers, wedge-ledge chompers, freshwater tree squeaks, and occasionally a will o' the wisp or little person through the forests and hills around Sebec Lake in central

Maine. The ice fishing community seems to have kept alive some fearsome critters as well. While investigating the snow snake, it was heartening to learn about a newly discovered fearsome critter they have found called the ice hornet.

My original intent in writing this book was only to include fearsome critters and Old World immigrant creatures, like sea serpents, lutins, mermaids, and the werewolves known as *loup garou*. But as I found more and more connections and hybridizations between these and native Wabanaki creatures, I found it impossible to leave them out. The Wabanaki are a Native American confederacy of five separate nations all belonging to the Algonquin language and cultural group. From north to south along the Atlantic Coast, these include the Micmac and the Maliseet in southeastern Canada, as well as the Passamaquoddy, Penobscot, and Abenaki of northern New England. Historically their territory included the area from the St. Lawrence River west to Lake Champlain and south to the Merrimack River in Massachusetts.

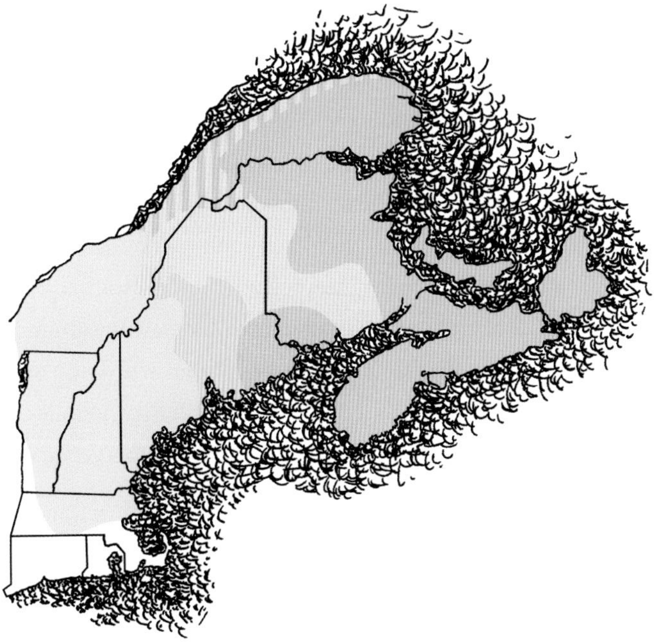

This map illustrates the territories of the five Wabanaki nations in the eighteenth century: Micmac (purple), Maliseet (blue), Passamaquoddy (brown), Penobscot (pink), Abenaki (green).

Originally, I believed the indigenous creatures might be only the Wabanaki's to share, and indeed they are. But the more I thought about it, and the more I learned about these creatures, the more important it became to me to include these wondrous creatures and beings. The Wabanaki are a huge part of Maine's story, and I believe their part should be told. All too often, Native American cultures and their role in our history have been forgotten or belittled; leaving them out would be unfair and irresponsible. Native people have lived here for thousands of years. The depth of connection and understanding native cultures have with the land is invaluable and cannot be overstated. Many non-Wabanaki authors of the nineteenth and twentieth centuries felt much the same, and I am deeply indebted to these people for their tireless work and writings. They include Frank Speck, Charles Leland, Abby Alger, Fannie Hardy Eckstorm, and Susan Stevens. Many of them predicted a time in the not too distant future when many of these Wabanaki people and their rich stories would be gone forever. Indeed, like most native peoples, the Wabanaki and their culture suffered greatly from colonization, but, unlike many of the East Coast's native peoples, the Wabanaki survived and have rekindled their confederacy and culture. While still struggling from the ongoing effects of colonization, they are healing and growing—in fact, by all reckonings, they are stronger nations now than they have been in a hundred years. So, with full acknowledgment and respect, I include their creatures here as part of a complete guide to the wondrous beings of this area. Inclusion of their culture in this volume is meant in a spirit of celebration and connection. While I have done my best, I likely have made some mistakes, for which I apologize. For those whose interest is piqued in this area, I encourage you to seek out and experience the Wabanaki culture directly from these people who are very much still alive. There are many fine events, museums, storytellers, teachers, and modern books where one can learn more (Appendix C shares some of these resources).

Some might wonder how the creatures such as the ones in this book could be real and yet remain unknown to science. I can't fully explain this situation, though it is safe to say that these creatures live at the edge of our reality. Perhaps they live in a reflection of our world, one we can only visit in dreams and stories. Or perhaps they have some special adaptation that allows them to live outside of regular space and time. As Abenaki storyteller Joseph Bruchac says in his book *Night Wings*, perhaps "it is because they live most of the time in that other reality, the one that flows between past and present. They know the trails that lead back and forth between then and now." For them, maybe time and reality are not a straight line, but rather something that keeps happening. Maybe there are layers within our reality that they can access, but we usually cannot. However, you don't have to be special to find these creatures—they're here if you know how to look. I have found that with a little knowledge, the right intention, and enough time, anyone can learn to venture out and meet these wondrous creatures.

It's important to know that these creatures are found mostly in wild places—places where mystery can still be found. But not all wild places are equal; these creatures are often found in liminal spaces. These are places with two natures, places that exist as an in-between, not quite one or the other. A beach, for instance, is neither fully land nor ocean; a newly cut forest is a place that is partway between wild and settled. Throughout human history, these in-between spaces have been considered magical places where otherworldly things can happen. So it is not a coincidence that many of these creatures are found in wild liminal spaces, or places with two natures: marshes, bogs, shores, waterfalls, frozen lakes, abandoned fields, and crossroads. A little bit of magic is needed to see these creatures, but we all have magic inside ourselves, for the key to unlocking most magic starts with imagination.

The only parts of this book that are solely from my imagination are the quotes from my great-great-grandfather Burton Marlborough Packard's journal. He undoubtedly knew these creatures, though he never got a chance to write anything down about them. Born in 1866 to a Searsport master shipbuilder, as a young man he tried his hand as a lumberman, but he spent most of his adult life as an owner-operator of a small lakefront hotel and cottages on Sebec Lake, where he catered to both vacationers and locals who made their living off the land. He and his family saw and heard it all, including these creatures whose stories have been passed down through the generations to me.

My biggest regret in my research is that I didn't start it sooner, before so many of those who knew these creatures best were gone. So often when I thought I was hot on the trail of a creature, my sources would respond with "I don't know those; I think they might be extinct around here." My other great regret is that I never could catch sight of the elusive Youmistit, and though many other people claim to have seen it, I still don't know much about it. If you see one, let me know. But in the meantime, I hope this field guide serves you well. Stay safe, and happy hunting out there! And please, let me know what you find—I'd love to hear about it.

# AGROPELTER

**Fearsome Critter of the Lumberwoods**
(*Anthrocephalus craniofractans*)

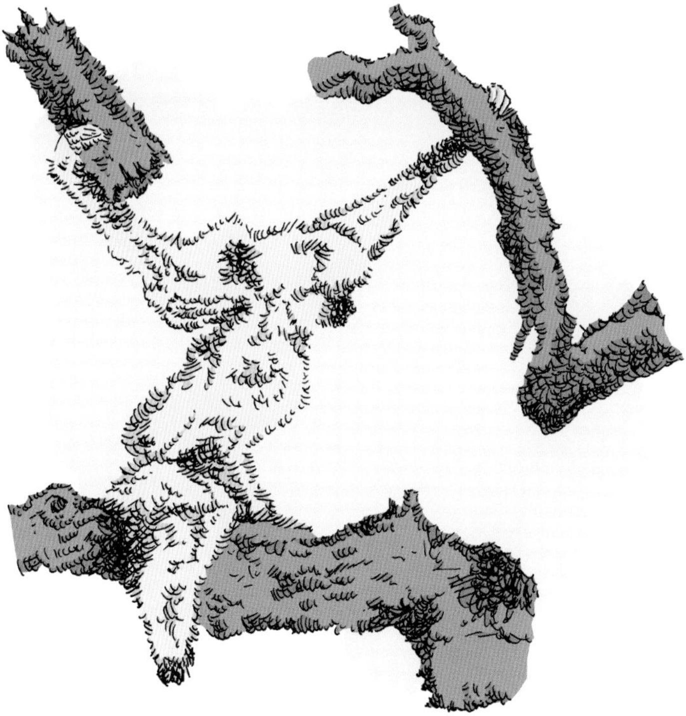

**THE AGROPELTERS** are mean little ape-like creatures with the dangerous habit of throwing dead branches at people who disturb them. Their favorite target seems to be lumberjacks' heads, but anyone

Sometimes called the "widow maker," many a lumberman has met his end after being brained by an agropelter-thrown branch.

walking past their tree (or even a stiff breeze) can set them off. They are surprisingly strong and can throw branches that weigh more than they do, with deadly accuracy. Minnesota state forester William Cox described their deadly habit this way: "The unfortunate is usually found smashed or pinned by a dead branch and reported as having been killed by a falling limb." But there can be no doubt that this vengeful creature is responsible. Over the years, so many people have been killed by these creatures that they have sometimes been called the "widow maker."

These ill-tempered apes make their homes high in dead hollow trees. They are active throughout the year and can be found in the north woods from Maine to Oregon. Despite their wide range, agropelters are rarely noticed, and few people who become their targets survive to tell the tale. Making them even more elusive, they are entirely tree dwelling and prefer

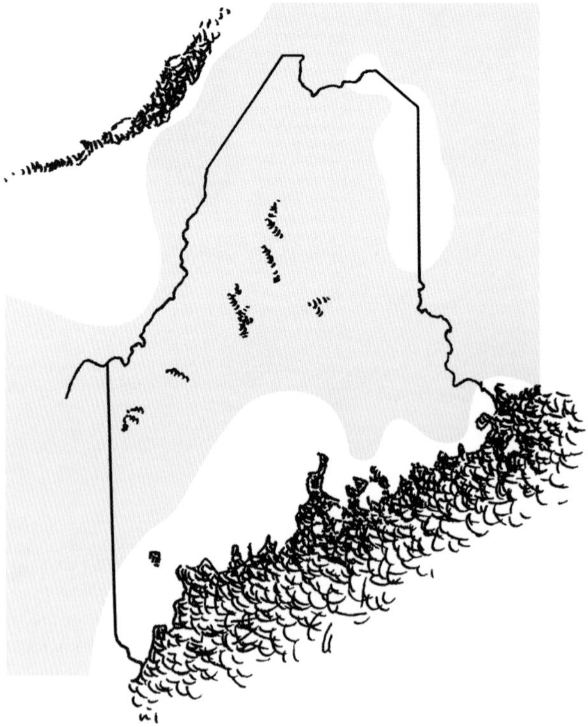

Agropelters can be found throughout the region in areas of continuous woodland.

to never touch the ground. They travel by using their long arms to swing from tree to tree, much like a gibbon. Agropelters never drink water from lakes or streams; instead, they get all the moisture they need from rotten wood, tree sap, and snow. Agropelters often take over nests of their favorite prey—owls and woodpeckers—and enlarge the cavities by eating the rotten wood. This strange creature has a unique four-year reproductive cycle and gives birth only on February 29. They always have an odd number of pups, typically three or five.

> *"I covered some new ground in my rambling today, but I won't be returning to the spot. The old forest there is apparently infested with agropelters. Three or four dead branches came crashing down within a few feet of me. And I could hear the low cackling of the widow makers themselves as I made a mad retreat."*
>
> —Burton Marlborough Packard, 1897

# BIGFOOT

## Cryptid Creature

Since the late 1950s, the bigfoot has been the most well-known and often-sighted mysterious creature in North America. But even before this time, there were persistent reports of large footprints and giant hairy wildmen in the wilderness.

**WHILE BIGFOOT** (or *sasquatch*, from the Sts'ailes language) is probably the most well-known mysterious creature in North America, it is only occasionally reported in the Northeast. These tall, ape-like creatures walk on two legs and are fairly intelligent. Some describe bigfoot as a missing link between humans and apes. These bipedal apes have human-like faces and muscular eight- to ten-foot-tall bodies covered with long dark hair and a pungent smell. They are shy and secretive and keep to the deep woods. The most frequently noted evidence of their existence are large footprints, howls, log knocking, brush-pile dens, and traces of hair they leave behind.

Maine certainly has enough forested land to hide a population of bigfoot. While there have been relatively few, reports of sightings have been occasional but persistent going back to colonial times. Recent Maine sightings have gotten little press and have mostly been shared on the internet by bigfoot research groups and individuals. Some of the notable bigfoot reports in Maine include details about them hunting snowshoe hares, traveling in pairs, and making brush piles near trees. One interesting account is that a pair of hairy, howling, bigfoot-like creatures invaded a campsite on Meddybemps Lake and stole some fish from two girls camped there. In fact, there have been a cluster of similar sightings in the area, which has earned them the nickname Meddybemps Howlers. Uniquely, many of the Meddybemps Howler accounts involve the creatures swimming in the lake.

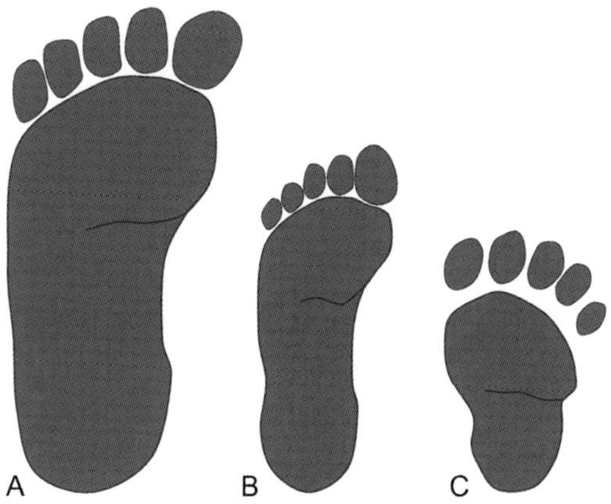


Bigfoot (A), human (B), and bear (C) footprints all have five toes—in each case, a print shown is from the left rear limb. Aside from obvious size differences, notice the distinct blockiness of the small toes, and the large toe points inward on the bigfoot, whereas the human large toe points forward. Bears, by contrast, have a shorter foot, the three center toes are somewhat clustered, and the smallest toe is on the inside of the foot in front of the ball of the foot.

There are several historic reports from Maine and the surrounding areas that also match the description of a bigfoot. The creatures in these early reports are sometimes called apes, gorillas, whazzits, or wildmen. The behavior of the creatures in these historic reports vary from peaceful and shy to savage and violent. For instance, very early European settlers in southern Maine recorded accounts of shy, hairy wildmen who were

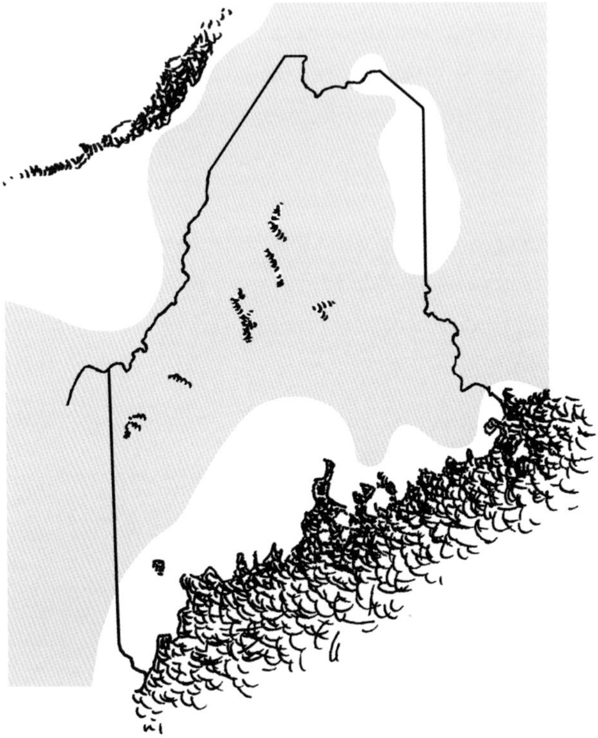

Bigfoot have been reported in forestland across the continent.

seen collecting plants in the fields outside of towns. And in 1886, the *Waterville Sentinel* reported that "a terrible wildman, ten feet tall, with arms seven feet in length, covered with long, brown hair," had killed a French hunter one hundred miles north of Moosehead. The creature in this report was said to later have been hunted and killed by the victim's friends and a group of locals.

Many Wabanaki stories also include creatures that are similar to bigfoot. In particular, the cannibal giants known as *chenoo* or *kiwakw* (see *Wendigo*) are six- to ten-foot-tall hairy humanoids. Like bigfoot, these terrifying creatures are known mostly from their howls and the large footprints they leave in the snow. However, unlike bigfoot, they are very dangerous man-eaters and more human-like than animal. It would be very unwise to cross paths with a wendigo. The *mikumwesuk* might also fit their description, despite the fact they are usually described as little forest elves. *Mikumwesuk* seem to have the ability to increase their size to that of a bigfoot and are sometimes described as being covered in hair.

> *"A guest asked me if I'd ever heard of a creature called 'sasquatch.' I hadn't, but what he described sounded a lot like the wendigo, except he said it was an animal and not an evil cannibal. I don't know why anyone would want to go looking for that kind of trouble."*
>
> —Burton Marlborough Packard, 1909

# BILLDAD

**Fearsome Critter of the Lumberwoods**

(*Saltipiscator falcorostrus*)

**THE BILLDAD IS** a mixed-up animal, with a hawk-like beak, big eyes, and a body and tail like a beaver. Its legs are long and powerful in the back and short in the front, much like a kangaroo. They are champion jumpers—a large male billdad can launch itself up to sixty feet. They eat fish and spend most of their time

These odd little animals are America's platypus. They are a sight to see, but they are only found in Boundary Pond, near Quebec, and you can't get there from here.

crouched on the shore, waiting for a fish to surface. When it spots one, the billdad jumps out and smacks its tail down hard on the water to stun the fish. The billdad then picks up the stunned fish and swims back to shore to enjoy its meal.

Anyone in billdad territory at night will likely hear their loud splashing, which sounds like a paddle hitting the water. If you want to see a billdad, paddling in a canoe or kayak is the best way to do it, as they prefer shallow brushy shore to open perches. This cover helps them avoid their predators, the great horned owl and the bald eagle.

While it is commonly believed that billdad meat is delicious, it's also known to be very poisonous, so few people have ever tasted it. In fact, the only known account of a person eating billdad told of an unfortunate

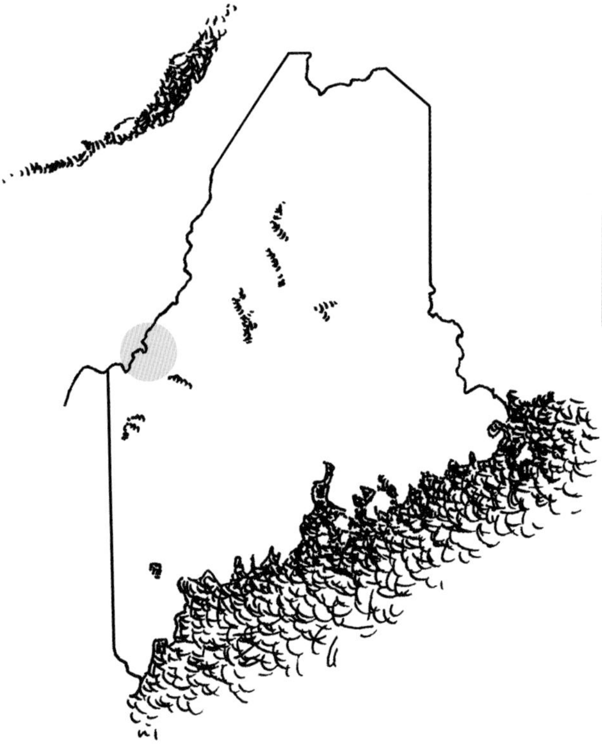

Billdads can be found only in Boundary Pond of Beattie Township.

lumberjack named Bill Murphy, of Ambajejus, Maine. After one mouthful of billdad stew, he froze up for a moment and then ran to the nearest lake and jumped fifty yards clear out into the water. He went into the water in a sitting position just as if he was a billdad smacking a fish with its tail. But since he wasn't a billdad, he sank like a stone and was never seen again.

> *"I was up to Boundary Pond, and there is really the most amazing creature there—the billdad. It was quite a sight to see, watching them silently jump out after fish, their legs held out front, and their hawkish beak and large tail silhouetted by the full moon. Then to land with such a splash, you would think a full-grown man had jumped in the water."*
>
> —Burton Marlborough Packard, 1911

# CELOFAY

**Fearsome Critter of the Lumberwoods**
(*Lynx horrificus*)

A phantom wildcat with uncanny ventriloquist powers, the celofay has been terrorizing people in the woods at night for years.

**THIS MYSTERIOUS** wildcat of the deep forest has the clever ability to throw its voice. This skilled ventriloquist can make its scream-like yowl seem to come from any direction. It uses this ability to panic its prey and then herds it in whatever direction it chooses, often in a large circle. When the prey is thoroughly lost and tired out, the celofay simply comes over and finishes the job. Of course, since the celofay normally stalks its prey for an hour or more, the best way to escape seems to be to ignore its yowls and head directly back to the safety of your home, camp, or even a vehicle. But then again, you never know with a celofay. Henry Tyron, director of the Black Rock Forest in New York State, tells us that one of these "can easily project his fearsome squall across a section, right up beside you, in fact. Or he can reverse the situation and toss his yowl into some distant cedar swamp while he stealthily stalks you with malicious intent."

Like its smaller cousin, the housecat, this creature seems to enjoy toying with its prey. Some say the celofay feeds as much upon fear as the animals and people it catches. It was first described by French Canadian lumbermen in Maine, and its name is derived from the similar-sounding French phrase *c'est la feé*, which means "of the fairy." Despite being a relatively small cat, the celofay's prey is mostly large animals such as deer, moose, bear, coyotes, dogs, and an occasional unlucky woodsman.

Oldtimers sometimes tell stories about a feline creature called the *lucifee*, which in many accounts seems to have several common characteristics

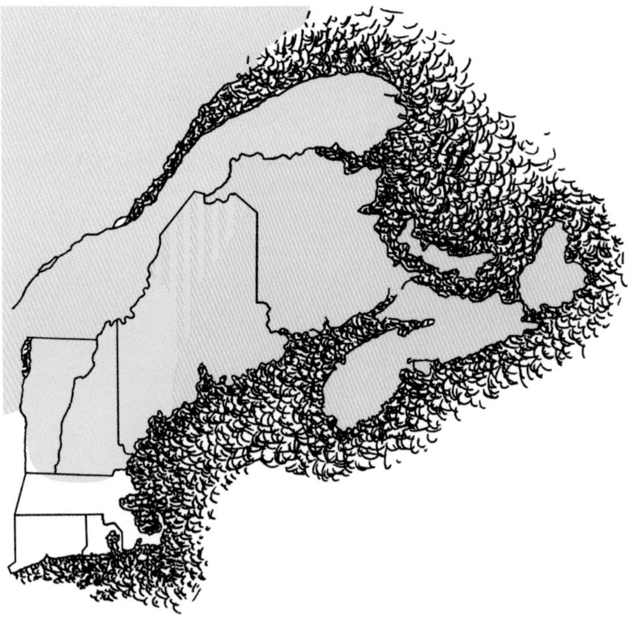

The celofay can be found in forests throughout historically French-influenced areas of Canada and New England: Acadian (pink), Quebecois (blue), areas of later migration (green).

with the celofay. In another report by T. H. Gray in Down East Maine, the oldtimers would say "while the lucifee never attacked humans, its nocturnal screams scared the daylights out of people in the area." And in central Maine, my great-grandmother used to complain about how the cries of the lucifee would come from all around and scare her when she was coming back from hunting at night.

The word "lucifee" is, however, just an English spelling of the French Candian word for the Canada lynx, which is *loup cervier*. This term is pronounced "lew-sir-vee," which, if you don't speak French, is identical to "lucifee." Literally, *loup cervier* translates to "deer wolf," which is how the long-legged cat looked to early French settlers. The Canada lynx (*Lynx canadensis*) is a northern wildcat that lives in northern Maine and Canada, where the snow is too deep to support bobcat populations. While it does have a terrifyingly eerie call, it only makes that sound during mating season and during territorial disputes. Canada lynx are not dangerous to humans; they hunt snowshoe hares almost exclusively.

> *"Even though I know all I need to do is ignore them, the celofay never fail to scare me while I'm walking home at night."*
>
> —Burton Marlborough Packard, 1899

# COME-AT-A-BODY

## Fearsome Critter of the Lumberwoods

(*Quadrupes inprovisus*)

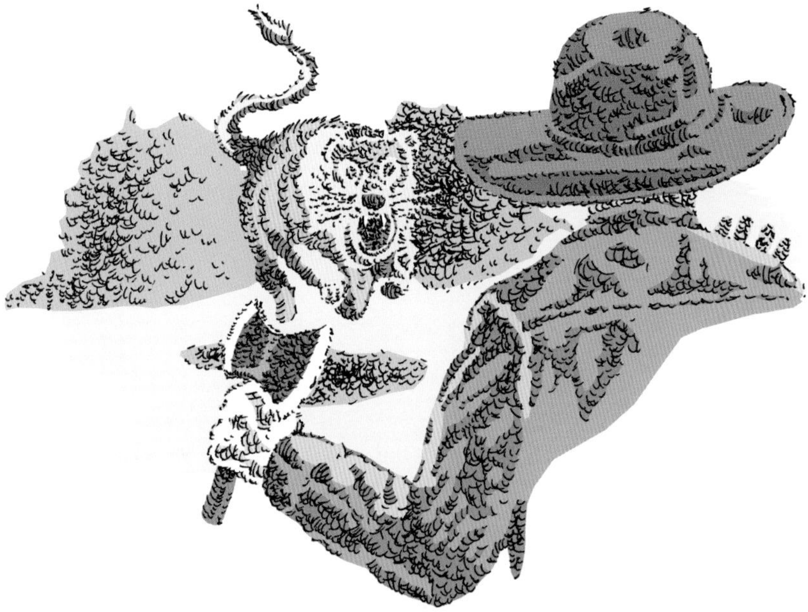

**MOST ANIMALS** run away from humans, but the come-at-a-body charges at anyone who comes near. The come-at-a-body is a fearless fellow with an attitude ten times the size of his little body. Many a brave woodsman has been sent running from these little guys. The meeting usually goes

The come-at-a-body is cute and fluffy, yes, but its snarling charge will make even the most steadfast explorer retreat in surprise.

something like this: You're just hiking along, minding your own business, when suddenly up ahead some little shrub erupts in a thrashing, hissing, spitting ball of terror. Then the snarling little creature comes right at you like a demon. At this point, most people run, and the come-at-a-body is happy to chase for a while, but for those brave enough to hold their ground, the come-at-a-body always stops a few inches away. Then, as a parting gift, he squeezes out a nasty, musky odor from his backside as he retreats into the brush.

Despite its bad attitude, the come-at-a-body is actually a cute little herbivorous mammal. It's a bit like a woodchuck, but with a short stubby body and flat face with large eyes. It has green whiskers and a pattern on its belly (or sometimes its back) that looks a bit like a dollar sign. Its

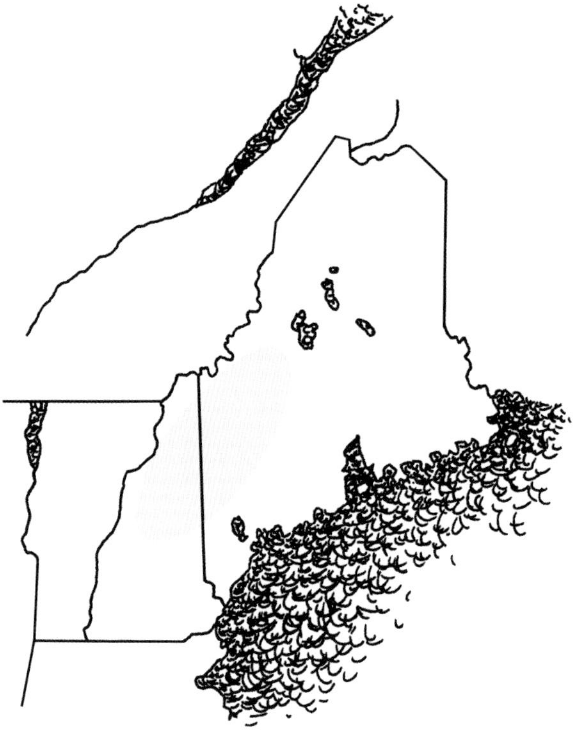

The come-at-a-body is found only in the White Mountains of New Hampshire and southern Maine.

fur is as soft as a kitten's, but most people don't get a chance to touch it. The male come-at-a-body has a slotted ball of fused hair on its tail that it whips around to create a loud moaning or whistling sound. It uses this sound while charging and as a mating call. Most people who have seen a come-at-a-body are too startled to notice much about their legs, but well-known White Mountains guide Joe Dodge claims that some of these little creatures have longer legs on one side of their bodies than the other. This characteristic helps them walk more easily on the steep slopes of the mountains where they live.

The come-at-a-body is found only in the steep White Mountains of New England, but it's quite similar to a burrowing creature found in Wisconsin called the sidehill dodger. The dodger also has uneven legs to accommodate the uphill and downhill sides. Perhaps they are both related to the much larger (and less startling) sidehill gouger.

*"I nearly messed my pants when that little fellow came tearing out of the bushes at me. And I did in fact scream like I was a schoolgirl being murdered by a bear. Old Sam must have known the little beast lived hereabouts because he insisted I go first and nearly fell over laughing at the whole incident."*

—Burton Marlborough Packard, 1911

# DING-BALL

## Fearsome Critter of the Lumberwoods

(*Felis caudaglobosa*)

**THE DREADED** ding-ball is a large nocturnal panther whose last tailbone is a large, smooth ball-shaped bone. No skin covers this deadly weapon, which the ding-ball swings at the skull of its prey. Ding-balls only eat large

Unsuspecting lumbermen were often lured out into night by the human-like calls of the ding-ball. Their reward was to be cracked in the head by the cat's tail.

animals, and many individuals seem to feed exclusively on humans. These big cats do not stalk or pounce on their prey like other large cats. Instead, they are skilled vocal mimics and can copy many sounds to attract their prey. When hunting people, they typically sing with a lovely human voice in an attempt to lure unsuspecting victims from their cabins or tents. They can be quite persistent, sometimes singing all night in hopes of a meal. If one does lure a victim out, it'll be waiting close by so it can attack with its deadly accurate tail. In fact, there have been no recorded instances of a person or animal surviving a blow from a ding-ball's tail.

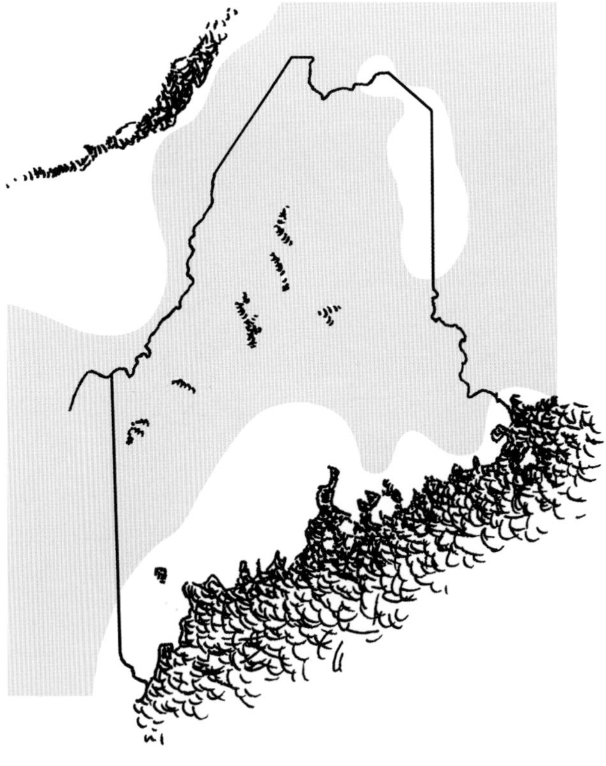

Historically the ding-ball could be found throughout the Maine lumberwoods.

During mating season, the males use their tails to drum on large hollow logs in an effort to attract a mate. This animal was once quite common in the early lumberwoods, but today, as with most large predators, it's quite rare. Outside of New England, this animal is much smaller and known as the ball-tailed cat.

> *"It was pitch black out; there was no moon when the singing started. It kept up all night, soft and soothing like. Sam and I had no choice but to stay holed up inside our camp—we peed in a pot and slept with our guns. Neither of us was fool enough to go outside and get brained by that ding-ball."*
>
> —Burton Marlborough Packard, 1900

# DINGMAUL

## Fearsome Critter of the Lumberwoods

(*Saxicatellus vociferens*)

The dingmaul is a majestic and gentle mountain cat, content to lie about on rocks unless you make it happy or scared. Then watch out for its wildly swinging tail.

**THESE LARGE** cats are generally harmless to humans, preferring to run rather than fight. The dingmaul is built low to the ground and has a tail twice the length of its body, ending in a tuft of hair and a medium-sized bony ball at the end. Their tails are used primarily to break up trees and dead wood into small pieces, which they use as nesting material in their dens. The tail is also used to keep off biting insects and for courtship. During mating season, the male dingmaul attracts females by pounding his chest with his tail to make a thunking sound that can be heard for miles. The female uses her tail to beat any male she encounters. This practice ensures she has found a strong mate. Outside of mating season, the dingmaul is a solitary animal and highly territorial. Their call is a loud wail that warns off other dingmauls.

These large cats have short, thick necks, round heads, and tufted ears. Their bodies are long and slim, with short, powerful limbs and slick wolf-like fur. They are most often seen sunning themselves on large flat rocks—they especially like those with a good view. One such rock is even known as Dingmaul Rock. This well-known landmark is in New Hampshire along the Appalachian Trail between Mount Adams and Mount Jefferson. Well-informed guides warn their parties to be careful not to do anything that might make a dingmaul happy. This can be quite dangerous, as they swing their tails wildly when they're happy and can injure anyone nearby.

A similar creature called a splinter cat haunts the same White Mountains territory as the dingmaul. While unconfirmed in Maine, the splinter cat is a fearsome but dim-witted and hard-headed cat with peltin thumper–like tree-breaking tendencies. However, these creatures break tree trunks by jumping at them headfirst in a misguided search for food.

Some sources claim dingmauls only live in the White Mountains of New Hampshire, but this animal is also known in the central mountains of Maine. The Maine variant has a much thicker tail ending in a bowling ball–sized club. In Maine, it is known as a peltin thumper or plunkus. The sound of the wind in the trees makes these fellows run around in a circle like a dog chasing its tail. But their heavy tails knock the trees they bump clean over. Seeing a circle of tipped-over and broken trees is a sure sign that a peltin thumper was around. The tree-breaking habits of the dingmaul have in some places also earned it the nickname "kindling cat."

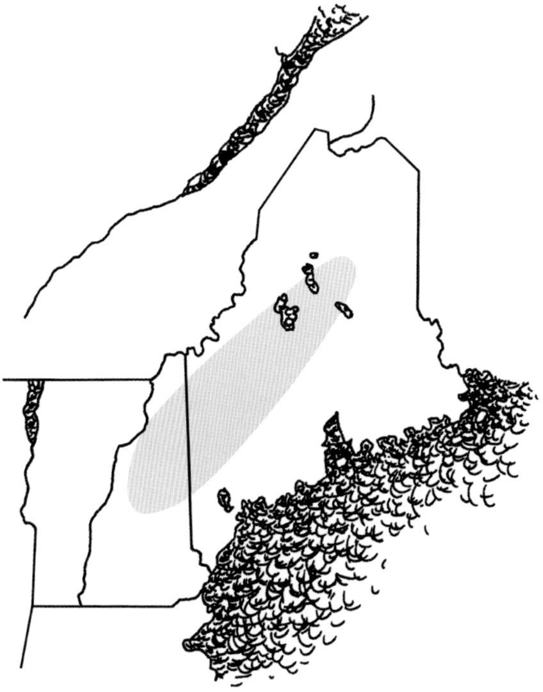

The dingmaul can be found in hills and mountains throughout central Maine and the White Mountains of New Hampshire, and perhaps beyond.

*"When I came to the clearing, there he was, big and beautiful, just lying there on that rock swinging his long tail from side to side and looking around. Our eyes met for a moment; he didn't have any interest in me, but I could see that it would be a good idea to keep my distance."*

—Burton Marlborough Packard, 1895

# DUNGAVENHOOTER

## Fearsome Critter of the Lumberwoods

(*Crocodilus hauriens*)

What it lacks in mouth, this reptilian predator makes up for in nostrils. It pounds its unsuspecting prey into a gaseous pulp, which it can snort up through its nose.

**THE DUNGAVENHOOTER** is a strange sort of northern alligator that completely lacks a mouth. But what it's missing in mouth, it more than makes up for in huge nostrils. Even without a mouth, this large reptile is a ferocious predator. It's an ambush hunter that likes to hide deep in thick puckerbrush. When someone walks near enough, it strikes out with its thick tail to knock its victim down. Once the prey is on the ground, it uses its tail to pound the helpless victim into a vaporous pulp. The hooter then turns around and snorts the pulp up through its nose and down into its stomach. It will eat almost any animal, but it especially likes the taste of people who smell like alcohol.

The dungavenhooter gets its name because it must snort frequently to clear its nostrils and makes a loud, startling hooting noise when it does. So beware snorting or hooting brush! Most people never see the hooter coming until they've been knocked to the ground. Any area of thick brush could hide one, but these animals favor wet areas like bogs, swamps, and shoreland.

Hooters were once very common in Maine and in the Great Lakes region—many nineteenth-century lumbermen fell prey to these animals. However, likely due to the extensive use of machinery for harvesting and the decline of lumber camps, few people encounter dungavenhooters these days.

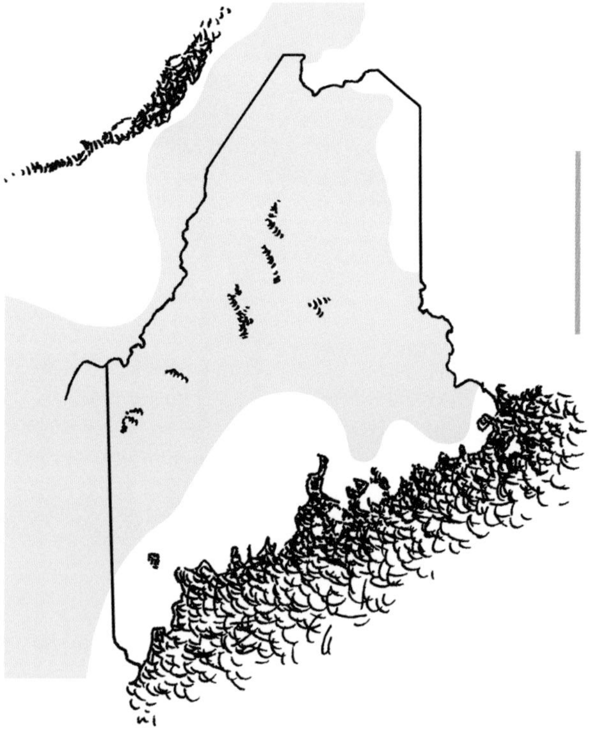

The dungavenhooter can be found throughout the lumberwoods of the region, though it is absent from New Brunswick.

This animal gets a mention in Leroy Dudley's *Chimney Pond Tales*, but what he describes is a mashup of several of the fearsome critters described by early lumbermen. In this story, Pamola and the hooter (as the combined embodiment of several fearsome critters) have a fierce battle for supremacy of Katahdin, the tallest mountain in Maine, which Pamola wins.

Interestingly, Dudley calls this creature of the North the dungarvin whooper. However, the name *dungarvin whooper* (pronounced "hooper") usually refers to a ghost—one of which in New Brunswick is perhaps the most famous of all. The whooper spirit is that of a lumber camp's cook, who makes himself known by whooping and hollering in the woods near the Dungarvon River, where he was murdered. Some claim that the victim was reincarnated as a panther or some other dangerous animal that now makes the whooping noise. But since panthers don't make any sounds that could remotely be described as "whooping," it's yet another link between the dungarvin whooper and the fearsome dungavenhooter. It is interesting to see how names often get confused and attached to new things as they move to new places.

*"So when the driver boys came in tonight they told me I wouldn't be seeing their foreman Johnny Cain again. They said he'd taken a shortcut through the old clearcut and he never made it back to camp. All they found was a stain on the ground, his boots, and an empty whiskey bottle. They figured it was one of those dungavenhooters that had done it."*

—Burton Marlborough Packard, 1896

# FAIRIES

## Old World Creatures

These playful spirits can be found everywhere in nature. Their shape and size may vary, but their curiosity and love of tiny gifts never does.

**TINY WINGED** fairies were once shy and rarely seen except by the most open-minded children playing in the forest. However, the fairy-house craze along the Maine coast has made them more familiar to people of all ages. These tiny people of the natural world emigrated to the New World with European settlers and inhabit all wild places in great number. In a way, they are the animated spirits of wild plants and places. Their clothing ranges from rich and lavish costumes made from woven spider silk and delicate natural objects to the barest covering of wisps and leaves.

These lovely creatures look just like little human youths with delicate wings. They are carefree and spend most of their time playing and exploring the forest. While they are nimble and fast on their own, they are often seen riding birds and squirrels. Many fairies enjoy keeping snails, insects, and other tiny animals as pets. Fairies also spend much of their time visiting and playing in the little fairy houses that people build for them. However, while fairies enjoy these little houses, few choose to move in permanently. Most prefer to live in intricate houses of their own creation inside flowers, trees, toadstools and even little holes. They use their magic to disguise their homes so that they appear to humans as no more than ordinary objects. In fact, most fairy houses are in places that seem too small to be a comfortable house, even for a fairy. But their magic makes it possible for these tiny homes to be much bigger on the inside.

Some fairies are quite solitary, while others enjoy the company of their fellows. On certain nights, such as the solstice, they all gather together for

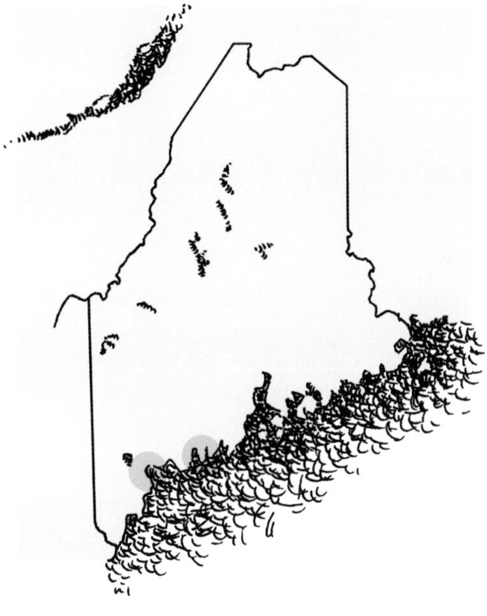

Fairies can be found everywhere but especially at the fairy villages on Mackworth Island (left) and the Gardens in Boothbay Harbor (right).

great festivals with dancing, singing, and marches. Rings of mushrooms mark their gathering sites. These circular toadstool growths are called fairy rings, and it is said that those who step inside are sometimes transported to a hidden fairy realm. Time moves differently there; an hour spent there is like a day here, and a day in fairy time is a year to us. Those who venture there and get to know the fairies often do not come back. If they do return, they are not the same. Some go mad, others become poets and artists, but all say our world pales in comparison, and they forever long to go back.

Fairy society is much like the feudal society of medieval Europe, with different classes of fairies ranging from regal royalty to humble peasants. Some of the noble fairies spend much time going on strange quests and solving mysteries so magical and complex that no human mind could understand them. But one thing all fairies love is to make bargains and play tricks on humans and each other.

They are masters of illusion, and in our world they are invisible unless they want to be seen. While it's not uncommon to catch a glimpse of a fairy from the corner of your eye, most people dismiss these glimpses as tricks of the mind or explain them away as small animals or other, more familiar happenings. Fairies are rarely harmful or even mischievous toward humans, and if threatened or insulted, they usually choose to simply vanish. If you are hunting fairies, your safest and best chance to see one is at a well-established fairy village where fairies have grown used to the company of humans. There are two large public fairy villages in Maine—both the Coastal Maine Botanical Gardens, in Boothbay Harbor, and Mackworth Island, in Falmouth, are lovely and worth a visit.

*"I think I must be getting a fever. For all the world, I'm certain I saw a tiny man riding squirrel as if it were a horse. It ran right across my path as I was walking back from the barn today; I think the little fellow even waved."*

—Burton Marlborough Packard, 1928

# GAZERIUM AND SNYDAE

## Mysterious Water Creatures

(*Gazerium vulgaris* and *Snydae minutus*)

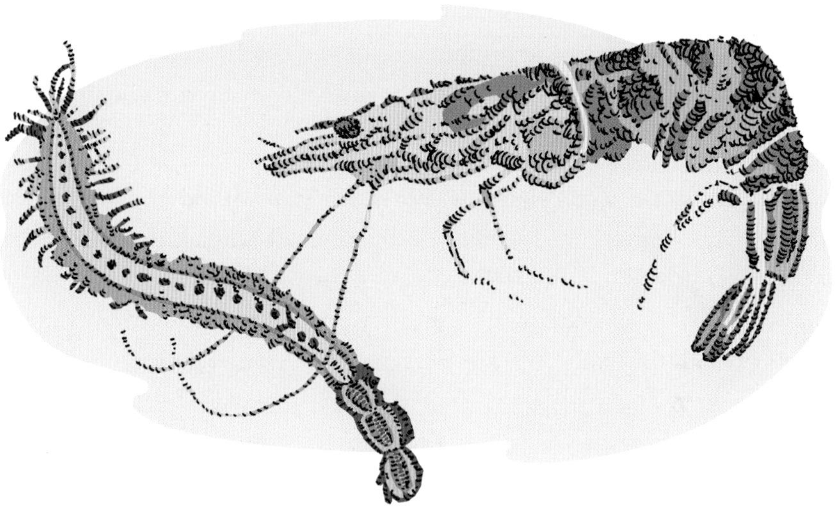

**THIS UNIQUE** pair of marine organisms has a very strange cooperative ecology in which each is the other's only known food. Found only in some tidal areas of the Kennebec River, the small gazerium and the tiny snydae are easily overlooked. First described scientifically in 1944 by Richard Kendell, these creatures were

Found only in the lower Kennebec River, these strange small creatures have a curious circular food chain. Gazerium eat only snydae, and snydae eat only gazerium eggs.

reported to be extinct, but they were in fact simply very rare. Today, due to improved water quality, they have made a small comeback and can again be observed in parts of their natural habitat.

The gazerium is a two- to four-inch-long shrimp that has only two front legs and a single rear leg near its tail. The snydae, by contrast, is a tiny, nearly microscopic, brightly colored swimming worm. The snydae swim together, forming small undulating clouds as they search shallow waters for their favorite food: gazerium eggs. The gazerium in turn swim about at the edge of the snydae swarms, eating them. The only time they stop feeding is to lay great quantities of eggs.

It is wholly unknown how this pair survives without driving each other to extinction. Quite possibly, there is another organism at play in their ecology. I suspect the bright color of the snydae may be due to the presence of photosynthetic algae living symbiotically on the skin or within the gut of the animal.

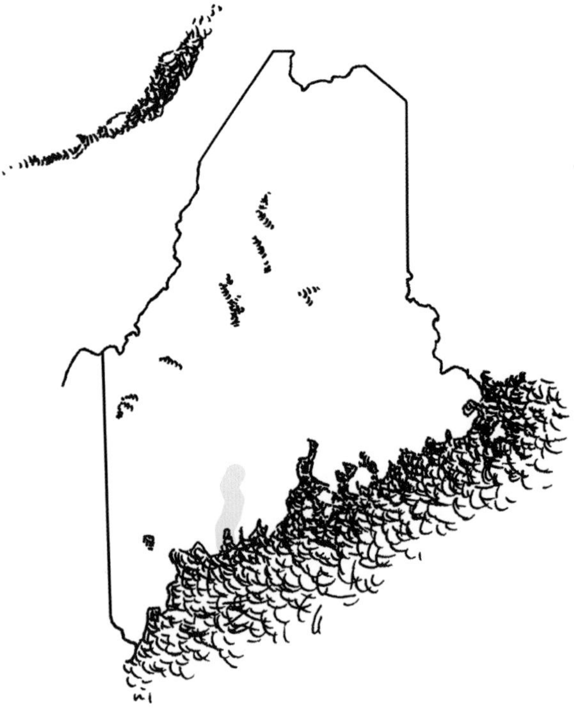

Gazerium and snydae can be found only in the tidal portions of the Kennebec River, from the Kennebec Bay north to the site of the removed Edwards Dam just upstream of Augusta.

In his original description, Kendell stated that the Kennebec Abenaki had eaten the gazerium deep fried in fat as part of their regular diet and that they tasted like fried potatoes and cocktail sauce. He attributed the gazerium's unique taste to their diet of snydae. However, since the Kennebec Abenaki had mostly been gone from the river for some 150 years prior, this account is unlikely. Additionally, cocktail sauce did not become widely known until the Prohibition era of the 1920s. So, it is unlikely he was quoting a historical reference. I can only assume that Kendell was speaking from firsthand experience with these animals and merely protecting their dwindling numbers by claiming that they were extinct. If this was the case, his plan has been fully successful.

> *"I was visiting a friend down to Hallowell, and they served the most unique shrimp I had ever eaten. It was larger than a normal shrimp and had only three legs. But most unique was the sharp and slightly spicy taste—they said they didn't add a single ingredient."*
>
> —Burton Marlborough Packard, 1912

# GIANTS

## Wabanaki Creatures

**ACCORDING TO** Wabanaki legend, long ago many types of giants lived throughout Maine and the surrounding area. Some were evil and some were good. At times, these giants adopted, abducted, married, and murdered Wabanaki people. Like the fairy tale giants of Europe, all of them were huge and imposing. The most well-known

Six types of giants can be found across the Wabanaki territory. From left to right: Magician giants like Gluskap of ancient times are the best known; thunder giants can be seen in the flashing lightning when they descend from their home in the clouds to hunt; stone giants like Katahdin can still be found living in their mountain wigwams; *kukwesuk* are a race of man-eating ogres; headless giants are rare but imposing; and the wendigo is a person who has been cursed to live as an evil cannibal giant.

type of giants in Maine are the magician giants. They typically lived like giant versions of the native people and took a central role in early Wabanaki creation myths. In their natural form, they were enormous—so large, in fact, that they could hang deer from their belt like a human hunter might hang a rabbit. Unlike their European cousins, they had powerful magic that allowed them to change shape and size and to do many other wondrous things. The most famous of these giants is Gluskap, the transformer, hero, and protector of the Wabanaki people. Gluskap spent most of his time ridding the land of monsters and evil giants. When the land was safe and free of monsters, Gluskap departed from Maine. He set out into the ocean from Mount Desert Island in his great stone canoe. He has not been seen since, but legend says that one day he will return when the need is great.

Today the only magician-like giants that remain are the great mountain giants whose eyebrows and cheekbones are made of stone. These giants live inside the mountains, which are actually huge, hollow stone wigwams with secret stone entrances. The best known of these giants is Katahdin, who lives with his family inside Maine's tallest mountain. One story about Katahdin tells that long ago he fell in love with a human woman and married her. It is said that she lives there with him still. Even today, music and lights can sometimes be heard coming out of Katahdin's wigwam. In a way, mountain giants are not just giant people but also the spirits of the mountains themselves. These days they spend most of their time sleeping, but spend enough time on a mountain, and you might get the opportunity to meet its giant when he wakes.

Another type of giant that still lives in the area are the *badogiak* or thunderers; they live in the clouds. These storm giants are sometimes known as the Thunder Brothers. They are a race of lovely, yet foreboding and powerful people. Like the magician giants, the thunderers can change size and shape. While powerful, they mean no harm to humans. Sometimes they even offer aid or adopt humans into their family. Most of all, these giants love to hunt. They often hunt a great spirit bird that lives in the southern sky, but their mortal enemies are creatures of the world below the surface: giant water serpents and *weewillmekq*. When the thunderers come to the Earth to hunt, they put on giant bird wings, and they can transform into great birds if they wish. Whether human or bird, the flap of their wings makes thunder and wind, and their arrows are lightning bolts. When a tree is struck by lightning, a stone thunder bullet (or *badogiak k'chi-gou-san*) can be found; if you dig around the roots, you might find one of these. They are said to be the most powerful of good luck charms. And if you look carefully during a storm, the thunderers can be seen for an instant among the flashes of lightning.

More than any other creature in Wabanaki lore, the *badogiak* corresponds to the important and widely known North American thunderbird, which rules the skies. Certainly these giants do more than the other large Wabanaki bird creatures, such as *Wuchowsen* (the wind bird) or *Culloo* (the large predatory bird that carries people away to eat them).

There are also other, smaller giants that can sometimes be encountered as well. The first is the headless giant, which can be seen on roads and paths late at night in northern Maine and neighboring New Brunswick. These

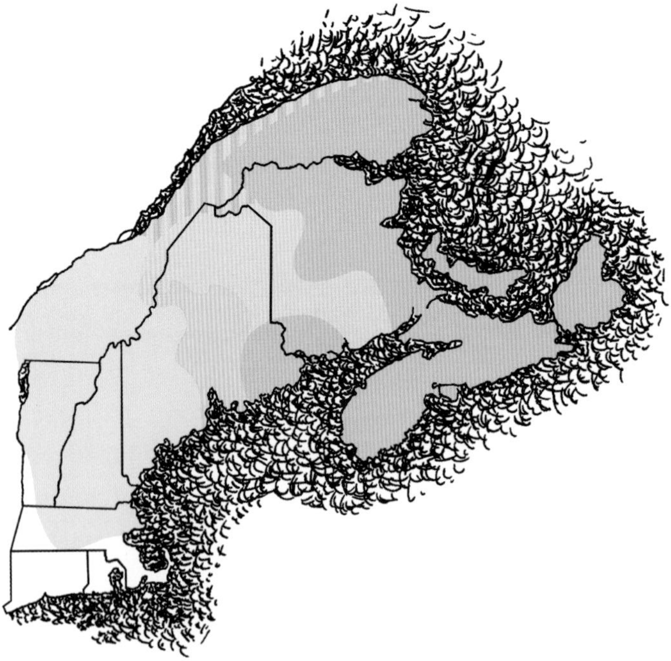

Giants can be found throughout traditional Wabanaki territory. The headless giants seem restricted to traditional Maliseet territory (blue), and the *kukwes* is found only in traditional Micmac territory (purple).

imposing figures usually avoid people and do not respond if approached. They are mysterious and little is known about them, but it would probably be unwise to aggravate them.

*Kukwes* ("kook-wess," from the Micmac) is a man-eating ogre with sharp teeth. This race of small, hairy giants is known for being both very greedy and very stupid. They are usually described as being twenty to thirty feet tall and strong enough to carry away several children at a time. Their name is the diminutive of *Kuku* (or *Gougou*), the Micmac word for a giant man-eating monster of the mythic age. *Kukwesuk* are sometimes confused with the wendigo (or *kiwakw*), which is a human that has been transformed through either magic or curse into a cannibal giant. They are also small but powerful giants, and they're always hungry. Their hearts are made of ice, and their bodies are covered in hair matted with sap, leaves, and moss. These relentless and cunning cannibal giants are discussed in more detail under *Wendigo*.

# HIDE-BEHIND

## Fearsome Critter of the Lumberwoods

(*Ursus dissimulans*)

This menacing and shadowy creature is what's behind you when you have that feeling you are being followed. They're fast, so no matter how fast you turn around, you can't catch a glimpse.

**HAVE YOU** ever had the feeling that something terrible was following you? And no matter how many times you turned around to check, the feeling wouldn't go away. That's a hide-behind, and this fearsome nocturnal creature only hunts humans. They are so fast and stealthy that whenever you turn around to spot them, they rush behind a tree or turn with you, staying just out of sight. This behavior of hiding behind its prey is how it gets its name. If the hide-behind wasn't so afraid of being seen, there would be a lot more to fear from it.

In the early days of Maine logging, these creatures were responsible for many lumbermen never making it back to camp. While there are fewer disappearances caused by hide-behinds these days, their stalking behavior seems to have increased.

They have adapted to life outside of the forest and can now be found in cities and suburbs, where they prowl outdoors around neighborhoods, backyards, and garages. They can even be encountered in the back seats of cars or vans.

Since this creature hunts humans, it should be avoided at all times. The best protection seems to be the smell of alcohol, which the hide-behind hates. In fact, there has never been a reported attack on a person who smelled like alcohol. It may sound silly, but some experts recommend carrying a can of beer with you at all times when in hide-behind territory.

While no one has ever seen a hide-behind directly (and lived to tell the tale), people often catch glimpses of them. From the people who have glimpsed the hide-behind, Henry Tyron has pieced together the best

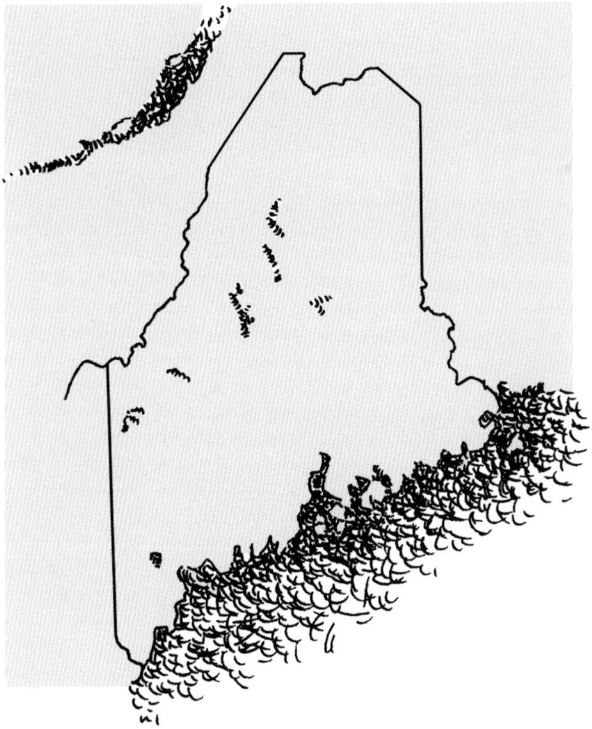

Hide-behinds can be found everywhere.

description known. It is a six-foot-tall, slender, dog-headed, bear-like creature that walks upright on two legs. It has shaggy black fur, strong arms, terrible claws, and a tail that curves upward. When it strikes, it shrieks and makes noises like a crazy person laughing, and it always attacks the belly of the victim with its claws.

> *"The hide-behind is the worst. I hate that feeling that something dark and terrible is following you through the woods."*
>
> —Burton Marlborough Packard, 1893

# ICE HORNETS

**Fearsome Water and Ice Critter**
(*Vespula glacialis*)

**THE SUREST** way to end a day of ice fishing before it has even begun is to drill into a nest of ice hornets. When an ice auger cuts into an ice hornet nest, these large and bad-tempered insects will erupt in a ferocious swarm to attack

These hornets build their nests in the ice. Woe to the ice fisherman who drills into one of them.

the fisherman. Their stingers are fiercely barbed and painfully venomous. Reportedly, the only way to get the stinger out is to use blackberry brandy, which quickly solves the problem.

There are only two ways to escape an ice hornet swarm. The first option is to run and jump into open water. While this method will certainly allow someone to escape the swarming hornets, it will also likely lead to drowning, hypothermia, or both. The second option, which has been used by at least a few brave souls from Millinocket, is to grab a hornet from the swarm and bite its head off. Supposedly, if this action can be repeated a couple dozen times, the rest of the swarm will get the message and leave you alone.

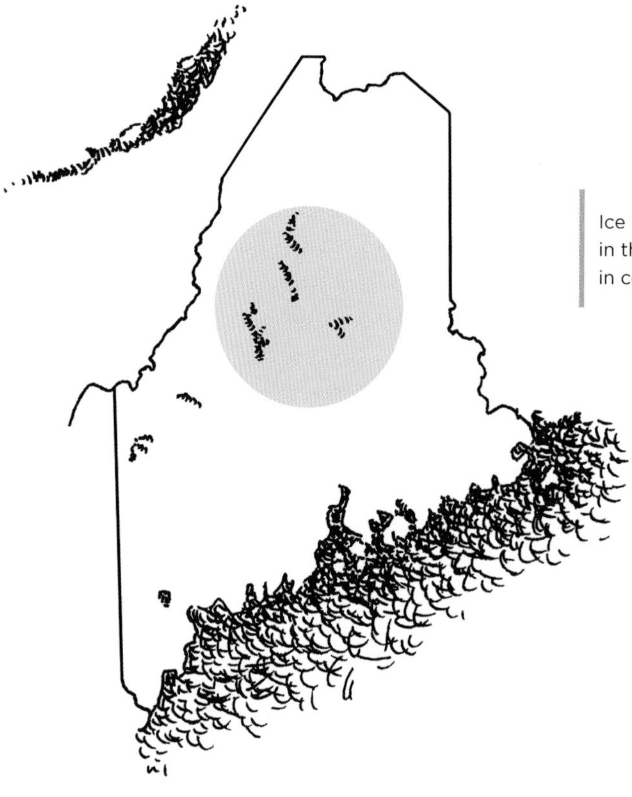

Ice hornets can be found in the ice of large lakes in central Maine.

Just as ground hornets are only active in the summer, ice hornets are only found in the winter. Despite their large size, they are never noticed unless disturbed. This scarcity is likely due to their excellent camouflage coloration. It is unknown how they survive the hot summer months. It may be that with the melting of the ice, the next generation sinks deep into the water and spends the summer months as aquatic larvae or dormant eggs.

*"Sam and I were out cutting some ice from the river to save for summer. We ended abruptly when the saw hit an ice hornet nest. We had to make a run for it and barely made it out."*

—Burton Marlborough Packard, 1915

# KAPUT BIRD

## Fearsome Critter of the Lumberwoods

(*Circumitio caput*)

**THIS UNFORTUNATE** species of bird has one wing that is shorter than the other. This imbalance means the kaput bird can only fly in circles. Typically, this issue is of no concern, as it just flies in slow, wide circles, lands on a branch,

This poor bird has wings of different lengths, so it flies in smaller and smaller circles until, *kaput*, it turns itself inside out.

adjusts itself, and takes off again in the correct direction. However, the kaput bird scares easily, and when it's scared it flies off very fast. This is where the bird runs into problems, because the faster it flies, the smaller the circle it flies in. When the bird fails to make any distance, it flies even faster. As all pilots know, this causes a phenomenon known as "accelerated circling," in which faster flying results in smaller circles. In the case of the kaput bird, the smaller circles result in faster flying, which result in even smaller circles, and so forth until the kaput bird is traveling at such fast speeds and in such small circles that—*kaput*—his head goes right up his backside. The unfortunate bird then falls to the ground in a lump.

Since the kaput bird always gains altitude as it circles, there usually isn't much to look at after they go "kaput." As a result, no one knows

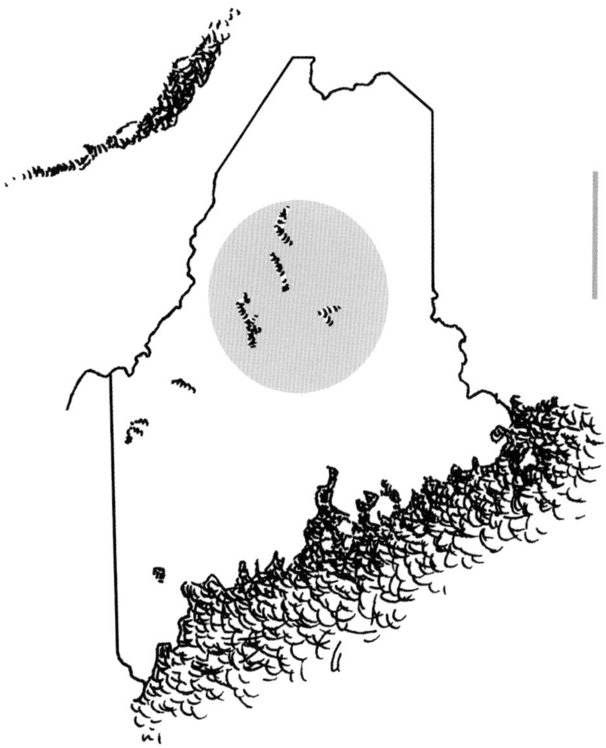

Kaput birds were historically found throughout the central Maine lakes region.

exactly what these birds look like. From the fleeting glimpses people get of them before they take off, they seem to be decent-sized birds somewhat resembling woodpeckers. Most experts agree that these birds have become quite endangered. They likely originally lived a peaceful life high in the canopy of central Maine's ancient pine forests, where they weren't disturbed. Once those forests began being logged, the peculiarities of the birds' wing length made their decline inevitable.

> *"The kids were out there driving those kaput birds crazy yesterday. They must have made a dozen of the poor little fellows go all inside out with their hollering."*
>
> —Burton Marlborough Packard, 1906

# LAKE SERPENT

## Wabanaki and Cryptid Creature

There have been hundreds of sightings of lake and river serpents throughout the region since prehistoric times.

**MOST PEOPLE** who swim and boat the lakes of Maine have probably given at least a thought to the mysterious creatures that might lie below them in the deep. Indeed, many lakes are known to have serpent-like monsters living in them. The Wabanaki call them *Kci-atosis*, or great snake, and have many stories about these giant water serpents. They have often been seen swimming with their heads a few feet above the water, followed by several humps undulating in and out of the water for eight to thirty feet. Their heads are not snake-like but variously described as horse-like, dog-like, or deer-like. Their massive bodies can be up to three feet wide, so they produce a noticeable wake behind them.

Their movements can easily stir up shallow water and make it murky—in fact, many lakes with serpents in them have quite dark water. Boyden Lake, for instance, is well known as the scene of a legendary battle between two lake monsters, which permanently muddied its waters. Because of this event, the lake is called *Neseik* (or muddy) in the Passamaquoddy language. Likewise, Fourth Machias Lake, another very murky lake, has more records of lake monster sightings than any other lake in Maine.

A notable exception to the rule that lake serpents are found in murky water can be found in Acadia National Park. The Lake of the Clouds (Sargent Mountain Pond) is said to be home to a great serpent, but this lake is so crystal clear and so deep that it has traditionally been known as a "bottomless" lake.

Aside from murky water as a sign of their presence, serpents leave long sinuous trails in swampy areas as they pass from lake to lake. They also dig dens in the banks of swampy bog ponds, and their burrowing has even been known to drain smaller ponds. These great serpents are most common in the Down East region, especially in the various chain lakes of the Machias and East Machias Rivers. They have also been seen in Sysladobsis, Spendic, and Skiff Lakes on the St. Croix River watershed. A large petroglyph of a serpent is carved onto the rocks of Grand Lake Stream, and several others exist on the rocks of Machias Bay. In Vermont, Lake Willoughby and Crystal Lake are also said to be home to long, dark lake serpents.

While lake serpents are uncommon and typically pose little threat to humans, they are not without danger. When feeding, very large serpents sometimes emerge from the water to catch animals. In one case at Pocomoonshine Lake, an unlucky lumberjack met his end this way.

While sunning themselves, serpents sometimes float partially on the surface, where they are easily mistaken for a log. This can be quite dangerous for anyone trying to drag a canoe or kayak over the "log." In many old Wabanaki stories, serpents hypnotize and seduce women into luring their husbands to the serpent in order to be devoured, though sometimes this phenomenon is associated with another creature called the *weewillmekq*.

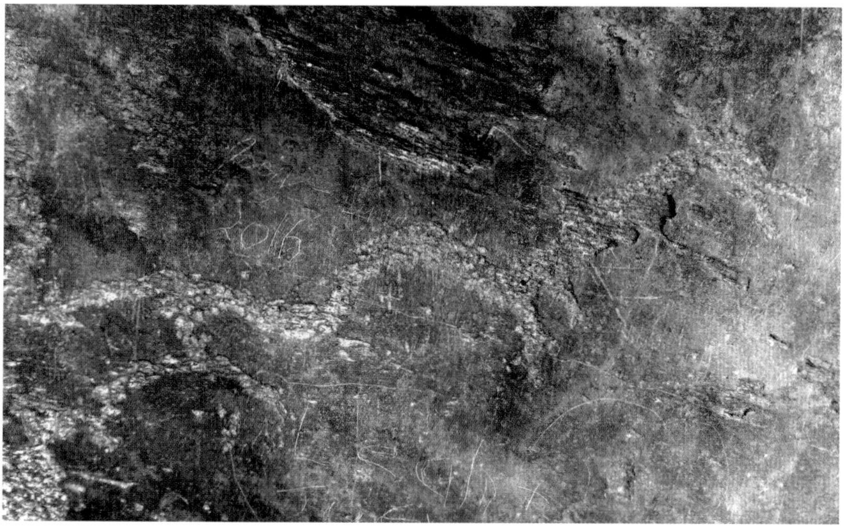

A horned dragon-like serpent is depicted along with dozens of other prehistoric petroglyphs of people and animals. These petroglyphs are located on a ledge in the Kennebec River in the town of Emden, approximately fifty-five miles upstream of Augusta.

Farther inland, lake monsters are described similarly but include reports of horns and fins on the creature. A prehistoric Wabanaki petroglyph on Embden Ledge in the Kennebec River depicts a serpent with limbs and horns.

These creatures may be unique, or they may be the same as the serpents formerly described, or they may be the *weewillmekq*, a creature that shares some characteristics with a serpent. Horned serpents have been sighted in Moosehead Lake in Maine, Kejimkujik Lake in Nova Scotia, and Lake Champlain and Memphremagog Lake in Vermont. They have also been seen in most of the large lakes in Quebec along the New England border, including Lake Pohenagamook, Lake Breeches, Lake Brompton, Lake Massawippi, Lake Saint Francois, Lake Aylmer, and Lake Williams. The best known of these is Champ, a serpent in Lake Champlain. Champ has been sighted hundreds of times and is widely considered the Loch Ness Monster of the United States. This creature is so well known that in the early 1980s both Vermont and New York passed laws giving legal protection to Lake Champlain's serpent. The Abenaki people of the area know Champ as *Padoskos*, which means "bigger than big snake."

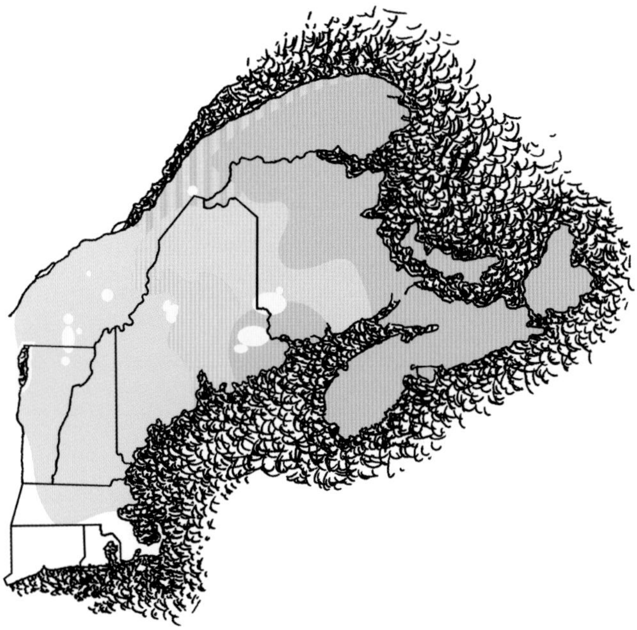

Lake serpents have been reported frequently in waters (yellow highlights) throughout traditional Wabanaki territory and beyond: Micmac (purple), Maliseet (blue), Passamaquoddy (brown), Penobscot (pink), Abenaki (green).

There is no doubt that sometimes lake serpent sightings are really logs, groups of otters, large snapping turtles, sturgeon, eel, or simply hoaxes. However, the long and widespread history of sightings leaves little doubt that lake serpents exist.

> *"There's no lake monster in* this *lake!"*
> —Burton Marlborough Packard, 1900

# LANDLOCKED WALRUS

## Fearsome Water Critter

(*Odobenus rosmarus* var. *chesuncookia*)

Deprived of their marine surroundings, these landlocked walruses are more dangerous than their marine cousins.

**THE FRESHWATER** walrus is known only from the remote Chesuncook Lake region. The landlocked walrus is a smaller relative of the better-known ocean variety. It is also perhaps more dangerous. Walruses are best known for their large tusks, which are actually overgrown canine teeth. They use these huge teeth not only to fight but also to haul their blubbery bodies out of the water and onto the ice. Around their tusks they have a mustache of stiff bristles that are not actually hair but sensory organs filled with blood and nerves. They use them to probe the muddy lake bottom for food. While a walrus will eat any animal that it can get into its mouth, its primary diet is mussels and clams. Its piston-shaped tongue can create a vacuum in its mouth that can literally suck shellfish out of their shells and even the flesh off the bones of larger animals.

Since walruses can remain submerged for up to half an hour and dive up to three hundred feet, they are difficult to track. When walruses do surface, they float with their head and neck above the water in a way that makes them look much like a person swimming. They have unique air sacs in their necks that allow them to float like this even when sleeping. These neck pouches also allow them to make many impressive and eerie sounds during mating season. Their large size and long tusks make them potentially quite dangerous. Landlocked walruses have been known to capsize boats or attack people with their tusks. They have even been known to break through ice to attack people walking on the surface above.

> *"I remember in the spring of 1861 that as I traveled on foot over a hundred miles from Katahdin Iron Works to the head waters of the St. John, I met many [lumber and hunting] crews coming out who usually had frightening stories to tell of the walruses and the danger I ran of meeting them."*
> —Manly Hardy, fur buyer, hunter, and naturalist (*Forest & Stream*, 1901)

Thankfully, landlocked walruses are very rare and seldom seen. Like the landlocked Atlantic salmon (*Salmo salar*), which is native to only four lakes in Maine (and also possibly Lake Champlain and Lake Ontario), the landlocked walrus is likely a glaciomarine relict—they were trapped in freshwater lakes some ten thousand years ago by changing sea levels at the end of the last Ice Age. However, unlike landlocked Atlantic salmon, which have been introduced into lakes around the world, the landlocked walrus has only ever been found in one lake and has become increasingly rare. In fact, in 1891, the last known written account of the landlocked walrus reported that it was extinct. Today, most likely only stories and fossilized bones and tusks remain of this bygone creature. However, marine walruses are still found along the Canadian coast, not far north of Maine.

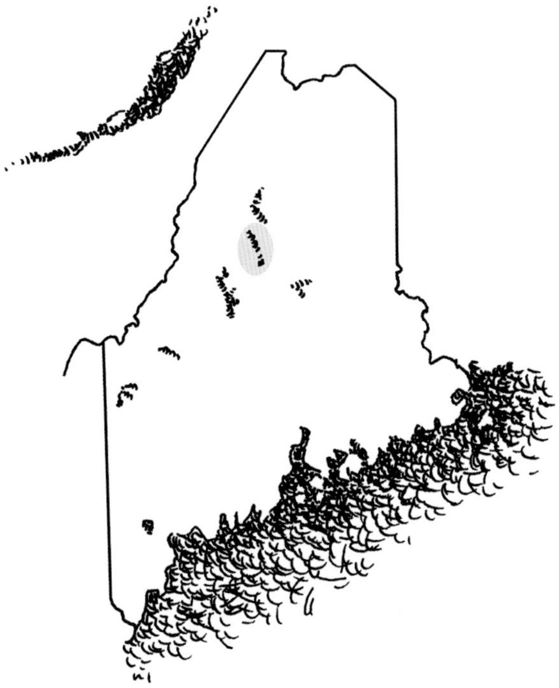

Landlocked walruses are found only in the Chesuncook Lake region (blue) of Maine.

*"I've always wanted to see a walrus, so when some choppers said that they had seen a few of the landlocked fellows in Chesuncook Lake, I had to head up there. When I finally made it, despite a couple days of paddling, I could not say for certain that I saw a single one."*

—Burton Marlborough Packard, 1908

# LITTLE PEOPLE OF MAINE

## Wabanaki and Old World Creatures

**HUMANS SHARE** the Northeast with several races of little people that all stand about three feet tall. Most of these little people are harmless and may even help those who treat them with respect. When offended, however, their revenge can be terrible. These races are similar to the small elves and leprechauns of European fairy tales. In fact, the lutins, which are well known in the French countryside, certainly arrived here with both Acadian and Quebecois French immigrants. The other four races described

Irish leprechauns were the scourge of Great Lakes lumbermen in the same way that Sock Saunders was to Maine lumbermen (T. C. Croker, 1862).

here are native to the forests and mountains of Maine and are frequently mentioned in Wabanaki tales. Both a translated name and Wabanaki names are given for these little people. In southern Wabanaki languages, plural words use the ending *-ak*, *-uk*, or *-eg*; inconveniently for English speakers, the singular ending is usually *-es* or *-sis*. Because of their secretive natures and powerful magic, all of these little people remain unknown to science. Many people on the East Coast are familiar with the gray-skinned, mischievous pukwudgies. These little people of Wampanoag and Delaware lore are found from Massachusetts south to New Jersey. They don't seem to venture farther north into northern New England or Canada.

It is unknown how the various races of little people that do live here interact with each other, but there are some striking similarities between them. I would not be surprised if they frequently interacted and intermarried with each other. In Canada, there are some reports of British little people called *bochdan* or *bauchan*. These hobgoblins correspond quite closely with the French *lutin*. Perhaps Sock Saunders, the gremlin who was the scourge of the nineteenth-century lumber camp, was one of these *bochan*. He was once so infamous that in many camps, if something went wrong, it was blamed on Sock. His antics included tripping people, stealing

If something went wrong in the lumber camp, chances are Sock Saunders was to blame.

tools, breaking equipment, setting fires, pushing felled trees in unexpected ways, and just about anything else that could harm a lumberman. No one ever saw Sock, and it was generally agreed that he was invisible. Whenever an accident was narrowly avoided, lumberman would often exclaim, "You didn't get me that time, Sock Saunders!" Most accounts describe him as an Old World Anglo-Saxon little person, but this fellow could have been any of the little people from the Old World or the New. It's easy to imagine that the little people native to these forests would not have taken kindly to lumbermen cutting down their homes.

## FOREST ELVES (*Mikumwesuk*)

### Wabanaki Creatures

The little *mikumwesuk* (or *mi'kmwesu*) are powerful wood spirits. They have long limbs and are sometimes said to be completely covered in hair. These little people are known throughout Maine and the surrounding areas

These small but very powerful little people like to keep to themselves, but they are always watching. Sometimes they're helpful if asked.

in Canada and New England, and even across the Great Lakes region. They live in the woods and are always curiously watching people. They can remain completely invisible and undetected unless they want to be seen. They are quite playful and most likely to reveal themselves to children. Sometimes a *mikumwes* befriends a young person and becomes their secret companion. These friends of a *mikumwes* are often granted great blessings or even secret powers.

The *mikumwesuk* have many other powerful magical abilities; for instance, they can walk into stone and sink into the ground if they choose. Their powerful magic also allows them to change their appearance at will. Sometimes a *mikumwes* will fall in love with an adult they have seen and appear to them in the forest as an attractive member of the opposite sex. Other times, when seen by people, they look like small humans about three feet tall and wearing fantastic clothes. But they can also change their height at will and can grow to the size of a small giant.

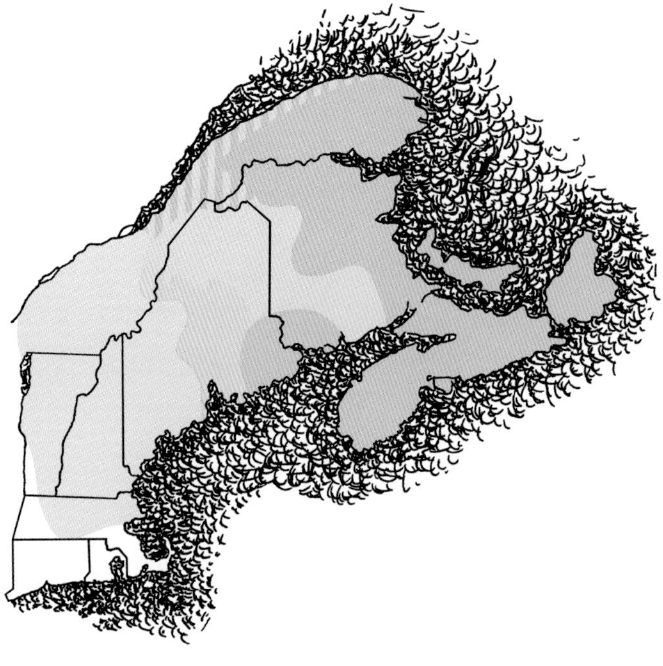

*Mikumwesuk* can be found throughout traditional Wabanaki territory: Micmac (purple), Maliseet (blue), Passamaquoddy (brown), Penobscot (pink), Abenaki (green).

Maliseet legend has it that the *mikumwesuk* are the descendents of Mikumwesu, a dwarf who was the brother and faithful companion of Gluskap. Like the legendary Mikumwesu, these little people have a generally good disposition and, when asked, are often quite helpful. They are particularly known to help people who become lost in the woods. But the aid they offer can go well beyond that. They can provide healing herbs, transport people great distances through the air, and tell the future. It is said that if one of the *mikumwesuk* tells you that you must do something, you must comply, or else things will go very badly. For those who know how to call them, they make excellent guardian spirits and can be recruited to guard people and places. However, *mikumwesuk* do not tolerate disrespect or trespassers, and they will quickly respond to insult or disrespect. For the worst offenders, their most dangerous magic is the evil eye, which can cause people to fall sick or even die. So, as with all little people, it is important to always treat them with respect and courtesy.

## LUTINS

### Old World Creatures

Lutins are powerful and fun-loving hobgoblins. They are similar in appearance to leprechauns. Originally from France, they immigrated here along with early French-speaking settlers. Acadians near the St. John River describe them as *du petit monde* (or "of the small world"). They are quite powerful and have many fantastic abilities, such as walking on water and entering through locked doors. They can become invisible at will and can transform into animals. They often travel around in the form of dogs, cats, birds, hares, or even snakes. They seem especially fond of taking the shape of black or white cats.

Lutins can be found living in lonely places like caves or near water. But like many Old World hobs, they often attach themselves to homes and farms, where they help out and sometimes play "harmless" tricks. Stray animals that adopt a home are often lutins, especially if they seem special

or have a unique appearance. Sometimes they help their adopted families with chores like caring for animals or cleaning. For those they truly favor, they can offer powerful assistance, such as healing the sick or bringing good weather. But once a lutin is disrespected, they offer only mischief. Some of their favorite tricks are filling shoes with peas or pebbles, sewing pants up at the knees, and turning the meat in soup into small stones. Lutins have a great love of horses, which they ride at night. They cannot resist putting braids or tangles in the manes and tails of horses. If the farmer treats the lutins with respect, the horse will enjoy good health, and only these "fairy-locks" will be left as evidence of the lutins' presence. However, if lutins are disrespected, the horse will be ridden hard and each morning will be rough, sweaty, and tired out. Luckily, lutins don't seem to have transferred their affection or mischief to automobiles.

Lutins immigrated here with the French. These little elves like to attach themselves to a home, where they can be helpful or mischievous.

Brownies from the British Isles are quite similar to French lutins. Illustration by Alice B. Woodward (1920).

In the winter, many Frenchmen in Maine would turn from farmers to lumbermen. The lutins followed them to the lumber camps, where they continued their antics with horses and also developed a knack for "tying" logging chains into impossible knots that could not be undone. The lumbermen found these chain knots all the more alarming because they often appeared while the chains were being used.

Should you get on the bad side of a mischievous lutin, there are certain ways they can be discouraged. Notably, they hate salt, and spreading salt in doorways and windows will often cause a lutin to leave. Likewise, they don't like holy water or religious objects. Another method is to spill many small seeds on the floor of the barn each night. The lutin will be obliged to pick them up one by one, and if this action is repeated frequently, they will become frustrated and leave. But as long as you treat a household lutin with kindness and courtesy, it can be quite a blessing to have one in your home.

Lutins are typically solitary, but in certain places at sunset they can sometimes be heard gathering together for a march through the land. Their invisible march is accompanied by the sound of flapping wings, rolling wagon wheels, barking dogs, ringing bells, laughing, and singing. In the early twentieth century, one of their songs was recorded by Sister Mary L. Fraser in an old Acadian area of Nova Scotia. The tune was lost, but the words went:

**Men's voices:** *Caribi, caribi,*
**Women's voices:** *Caribi, caribo,*
**Men's voices:** *Houpe li! Houpe la!*
**Women's voices:** *Caribi, caribo.*
**All together:** *Ah! ah! ah! tra, la, la. Oh! oh! oh! dri do do.*

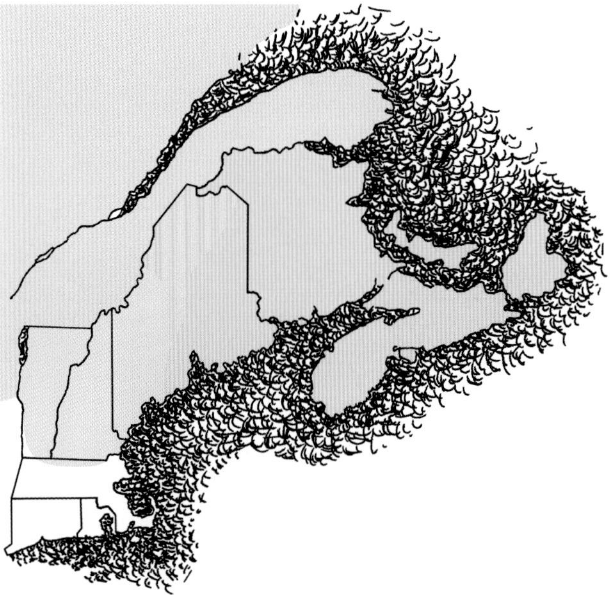

Lutins can be found throughout the region but especially in areas of traditional French influence and settlement: Acadian (pink), Quebecois (blue), areas of later migration (green).

If you are intent upon finding a lutin, you might try walking through the countryside singing that song. Perhaps one of the little people will join in with you. But as the old saying goes, "it's best to be careful what you go looking for, because you might just find it."

> *"I woke up this morning and found my horses had braids all through their manes. One of the Frenchmen told me this was sure to be the work of the little gremlin he called a 'lutin.' He said I was lucky to have one too, since they'll help look after the place. I could use the help, I suppose."*
>
> —Burton Marlborough Packard, 1894

## RIVER ELVES (*Manogamasak*)

### Wabanaki Creatures

Perhaps the most widespread species of Wabanaki little people are the river elves, or *manogamasak* (sometimes called *wanagameswak* or *wunagmessuk*). They are about three feet tall and have very thin, hatchet-shaped heads with narrow, close-set faces and enormous hooked noses nearly as tall as their head. They are very self-conscious of their ugliness and often cover their faces when seen. Perhaps for this reason, they are quite shy and avoid humans. If they do choose to meet a human, they are sometimes helpful and warn of danger. But beware: those who laugh at their ugliness are swiftly punished with mean tricks and curses.

River elves travel about in stone canoes that they can paddle in any water, even streams much too small or fast for human canoes. They seem

to be found throughout the Penobscot and Passamaquoddy parts of Maine as well as in southern Maine, Vermont, New Hampshire, and Canada. They are actually quite common but very secretive and rarely seen. They always avoid loud noises, especially engines and voices. If seen, they will quickly disappear under the water without a trace, either by jumping in or by submerging their canoe. Don't bother waiting for them to come back up—they can hold their breath indefinitely.

These shy little people are generally helpful, but they are very self-conscious of their ugly appearance. It would be extremely unwise to laugh at them or stare.

*"When he turned to me, I saw that he had the most beautiful fine long hair; but his face was narrow, with so long a chin that it rested on his breast. His nose was so big and broad that you could see it on each side of his head when his back was toward you. His eyes were very narrow up and down; and his mouth was the shape of a sharp A, the point running up under his nose. He wore no clothes."*—Sauk Ketch, Penobscot hunter (*Journal of American Folk-Lore*, 1915)

These days, *manogamasak* prefer to live mostly on smaller streams away from people, but they can still sometimes be found on the wilder parts of larger rivers. *Manogamasak* make their homes at deep pools with large rocks, where they decorate their rocks with crude, almost natural-looking, geometric carvings. Occasionally they can be seen on the shores near such places singing and dancing. Their favorite song has a sound like "*Hol! Hol!*" If you wish to see one of the *manogamasak*, find a lonely stream bank and sit quietly for a couple of hours.

They spend great amounts of time at night carving their homes and building with clay. Their clay sculptures can be quite intricate and can look like any familiar object: balls, animals, wheels, buttons, or even people. Important messages can be learned by those who study and understand *manogamasak* markings and clay sculptures. Others claim that if you find one of their clay figures or shapes on the shore, it will bring you very

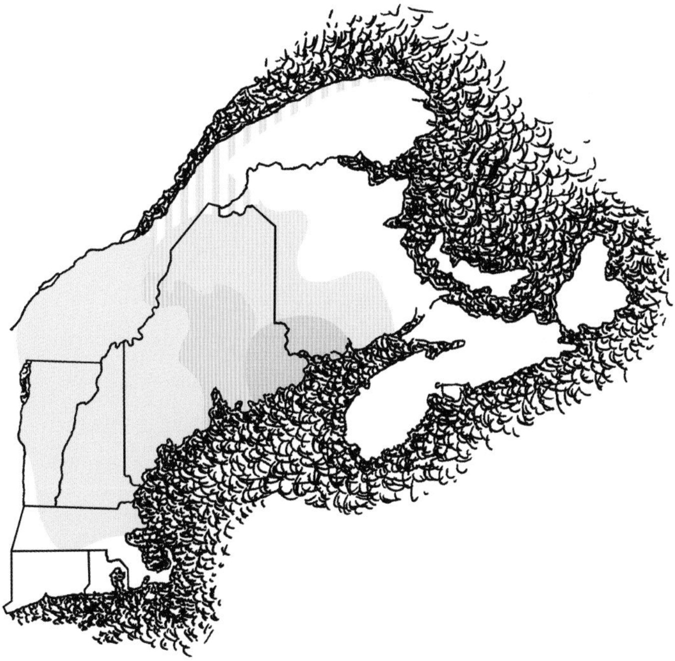

*Manogamasak* can be found on rivers and streams throughout traditional Wabanaki territory: Maliseet (blue), Passamaquoddy (brown), Penobscot (pink), Abenaki (green).

good luck—especially, perhaps, if you eat one! Formerly, their sculptures and markings were well known at the neck of Cape Jellison peninsula in Stockton Springs, West Grand Lake near Princeton, Taconnet Falls on the Kennebec River in Waterville, the islands south of Roque Bluff, the Hampden Narrows, and elsewhere in the Penobscot River and its tributary Kenduskeag Stream. They are also known at the Connecticut River and Button Bay in Vermont's Lake Champlain, which is named after the button-like shape of their small wheel-like creations.

While usually harmless, sometimes these river elves are very protective of their territory and can be cruelly mischievous to trespassing campers. They use sticks to prop open the mouths and eyes of their victims while they sleep. This behavior is similar to that of the Spreaders, another type of little person known to the Abenaki in southern New England and Quebec. Spreaders claim sections of certain rivers as their own, and anyone they find sleeping there will wake hopelessly tied to the ground with sticks holding open not just their eyes and mouths but also their fingers, toes, arms, and legs. Spreader territory should be avoided at all costs.

***Clay Concretion Fairy Stones***

To the eyes of geologists, the clay sculptures of the *manogamasak* are ordinary stones classified as clay concretions. These unusually shaped stones can be found as inclusions within large banks of glacial clay that formed some ten thousand years ago. Stones like these form as calcium carbonate molecules collect on small pebbles or fossils. Many of these stones have characteristic layering that corresponds to seasonal changes; each new layer was formed as glacial melt added fine sediment and dissolved minerals. The clay banks themselves formed this way as well. As meltwater flowed into deeper water, it carried the fine-grained sediment, which finally settled to the bottom to form rich deposits.

The fairy stones made by the *manogamasak* come in many shapes and sizes. These clay concretions were found on a tributary of the Penobscot River.

These clay deposits can be found along coastlines and at the bottoms of long-gone ancient glacial lakes scattered throughout New England, Quebec, and the Maritime Provinces and even across Europe. Each deposit—even those near each other—seems to form stones that have a distinct and unique quality. Along the Connecticut River, for instance, these stones have a human-like quality, with a smooth texture and subtle rippling that makes them appear to have muscled limbs. There they are affectionately known as "clay babies." But whatever they look like, in nearly every place they occur, these odd clay concretions are regarded as "fairy stones," and they are collected to bring good luck. Perhaps the magic of these stones is in the way they so perfectly bring together the mystery of magic and the power of ordinary nature in such a beautiful way.

## SILENT ELVES (*Kiwolatomuhsisok*)

### Wabanaki Creatures

Little is known for certain about the secretive *kiwolatomuhsisok* (or *geowludmosiseg*). These dwarves look like children or little old men, sometimes with long white beards. They never speak to humans and normally don't help or harm them. These little fellows can be seen just about anywhere, wild or civilized. They even come into people's homes and camps and seat themselves for a rest, but even then they don't say a word. They are most often seen alone but sometimes can be seen in small groups. Some people believe that seeing them is a sign of the future. But there is much disagreement about whether their appearance is a good or bad omen. Some say that their magic is such that the very attitude of the human who sees them determines whether they will bring good luck or bad.

These native little people are quite similar to lutins, but they don't mind being seen and they never say a word.

*Kiwolatomuhsisok* can be found throughout traditional Maliseet territory (blue).

Some people believe that the many similarities between the *kiwolatomuhsisok* and the lutins are due to a history of intermarriages between them. They do look and behave much the same, and both are found throughout present and former Maliseet country in New Brunswick and neighboring Maine. Within this area, there was certainly considerable interaction between French Acadians and Maliseet, both before and after English colonization.

## STONE DWARVES (*Wiklatmu'j*)

### Wabanaki Creatures

The *wiklatmu'j* (also known as *wiguladumooch*, *eguladumooch*, and *pugulatamutc*) are the stone dwarves of the Micmac. They can be found living in far northern Maine and surrounding Canada. These little people are oddly proportioned; somewhat like a bullfrog, they have large bodies, small

arms, and thin legs. Despite their small limbs, they are unbelievably swift runners and strong enough to toss an adult human with one hand. No matter how cold the weather, they always dress lightly and go barefoot. It would be difficult to tell males and females apart except that the males wear their black hair in braids and women wear it down.

These little people live in caves, rocks, and mountains. The bigger the home, the more of them that live there. In interactions with them, respect and politeness are key.

*Wiklatmu'j* are known as stone dwarves because they make their homes in mountains, rocky hills, and even large boulders. Generally, the bigger the mountain, the more *wiklatmu'j* live there. Sometimes the entrances to their homes are through caves, but other times they can make the rocks open up like a door or a mouth opening. The largest populations live on Tracadegash Mountain near Carleton in the Gaspe' Peninsula of Quebec, and also in the mountains of Cape Breton, Nova Scotia, but they have been sighted as far south as Katahdin.

The *wiklatmu'j* are generally good natured and spend most of their time singing, dancing, playing games, hunting, foraging for plants, and writing on stones. Their voices sound like bird songs and typically go unnoticed. They can sometimes be seen traveling on water in their small birch-bark canoes.

Unlike most other little people, they are not particularly shy and in fact can be quite hospitable if greeted with respect. Beware entering their homes, though, as time moves differently there. To the visitor, a stay in a stone-dwarf home can feel like only a night; yet in the ordinary world, years may pass by. If *wiklatmu'j* live near your home and they like you, they may sometimes help with chores. But be careful not to offend these people or their homes. Disrespectful people will find themselves having many tricks played on them. The *wiklatmu'j*'s favorite trick is tying things in knots, especially hair or clothing. Those who do awful things to the *wiklatmu'j* may be cursed and have their property destroyed.

*Wiklatmu'j* can be found throughout traditional Micmac territory and south at least to Katahdin in central Maine. They are particularly well known from Tracadegash Mountain (circle) on the Gaspe' Peninsula of Quebec (green) and from Cape Breton Island in Nova Scotia (green).

# LOUP GAROU

**Old World Creature**
(*Homo sapiens lycanthrope*)

**THE *LOUP GAROU*** is an Old World werewolf that immigrated here with early French settlers—both Acadian and Quebecois—and it seems to have followed wherever they settled. Most people know that werewolves are humans

This man-eating werewolf has long been associated with black sorcery; it seems to occur wherever French communities can be found.

that can transform into large wolves or even rough wolf-human hybrids. In legend they almost always have black fur. These are not noble creatures; they are evil man-eaters with black claws and long fangs. *Loup garou* can hunt on two legs or four, but they are fastest when moving on four. They can even run down a train. It's a haunting sight to see them gallop along with shoulders held high on long, powerful arms and hips low above their thin back legs. The only sight more chilling would be to look up into their yellow eyes after they have chased you down.

Hunting only at night, they favor children and lone adults. They like to ambush their prey, often at bridges. If you are ever hunted by a werewolf, you are in for a battle for your life. But it doesn't take silver bullets to fight against a *loup garou*. They can be injured or killed by normal means. In fact, the surest way to save yourself is to draw blood from the creature. Doing so will cause it to change back into a human and run away. Some protection from werewolves can also be offered by religious faith. They are said to fear holy objects, churches, and consecrated ground, and some have even been turned away by the holy words of a faithful person. Legend has it that if you don't run from a *loup garou*, it will not kill you, but only leave you with a terrible wound. However, it would be foolish to test this story, for it is a terrible fate to be killed by a werewolf—they don't just eat the body of their prey but also the soul. For this reason, some *loup garou* have been known to dig bodies out of graveyards.

In movies, becoming a werewolf is tied to being bitten by one and changing during a full moon. Neither seems to be the case with the American *loup garou*, however. Here, becoming a werewolf is the result of a divine curse for committing terrible acts, like cannibalism. Black sorcery can also be the cause—when faced with tough times, some sorcerers place the curse upon themselves to gain the *loup garou*'s terrible strength and shape-changing ability. Legend says that one must forswear religion and be in a state of "serious sin" to become a *loup garou*. Not surprisingly, there is a strong association between *loup garou* and witchcraft. In Maine, both witchcraft and the *loup garou* were once said to have had their origins on Quebec's Isle of Orleans in the St. Lawrence River.

While the name *loup garou* (pronounced "lew-gar-roo") may seem strange for something as familiar as a werewolf, it literally translates to "wolf werewolf." *Loup* is the French word for wolf, and *garou* comes from the Old French word *garoul* or *wareul*, which shares the same linguistic root of the English word *werewolf.*

Perhaps even before the arrival of European settlers, werewolf-like creatures roamed the area. Many Wabanaki legends involve human-animal characters for which the boundary between species is unclear and transformation of shape is a common occurrence. And, of course, there are many similarities between the man-eating *loup garou* and the cursed wild cannibal giant known as the wendigo.

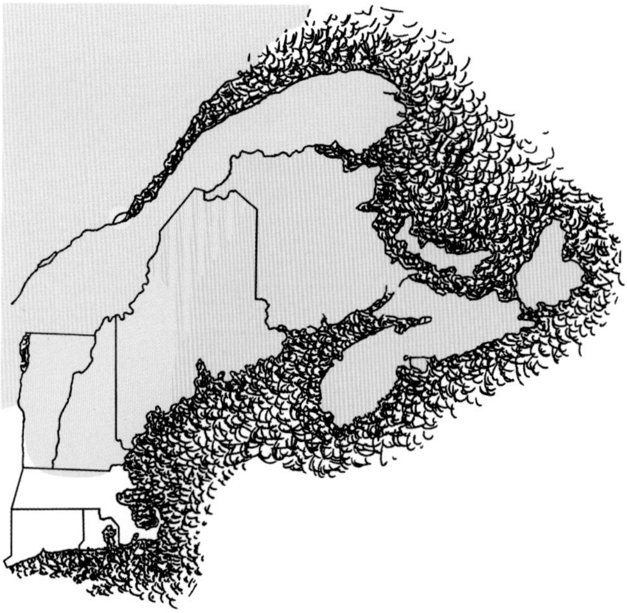

The Isle of Orleans in Quebec, Canada (yellow highlight), was once considered the epicenter of *loup garou* activity, but they can be found throughout all French-influenced areas of Canada and New England: Acadian (pink), Quebecois (blue), areas of later migration (green).

# LUNKSOOS

## Fearsome Critter of the Lumberwoods

(*Gulo gulo*)

**LEGEND HAS** it that the *lunksoos*, or "Indian Devil," was the only animal in the northeastern forests that Wabanaki hunters feared. They described it as more cunning and more terrible than any other predator. This fear was much repeated by the hunters and lumbermen of the nineteenth century, even though they had little

> Also known as the "Indian Devil," the wolverine was the only animal Wabanaki hunters feared. With the wolverine long extinct in Maine, the name *lunksoos* was frequently applied to other creatures.

concept of what this ferocious creature might be. Their accounts of hunting or being attacked by this creature describe it variously as a cougar, a lynx, a bigfoot-like creature, or a wolverine. In fact, confusion still exists regarding what this creature is or was. However, it is almost certainly the wolverine (*Gulo gulo*). At three feet long and up to forty pounds, it is the largest member of the weasel family and resembles a small bear. With its large teeth and claws, and an even bigger attitude, it is no wonder that it was so respected by Wabanaki hunters.

The wolverine is a predator and scavenger across the northern forests and tundra in North America. Built for winter, its large feet and claws allow it to run on top of snow. However, it is not fast and prefers to hunt by pouncing on its prey from trees and rocks. It hunts all animals, even those many times its size. The wolverine's fearless determination and terrible growls allow it to steal food from predators much larger than itself, and it has a bite powerful enough to crush bone or bite through frozen meat. It has even been known to walk into a hunter's camp and ransack it while scavenging for food. In John Giles's memoir of his six-year captivity among the Maliseet, he recorded some native sentiments about this creature. These early writings shed some light on both why the Wabanaki thought the creature a devil and how European settlers could easily confuse it with a cat.

> *"The wolverine is a very fierce and mischievous creature, about the bigness of a middling dog but with short legs, broad feet, and very sharp claws, and in my opinion may be reckoned a species of cat. . . . These wolverines go into wigwams which have been left for some time, scatter things abroad, and most filthily pollute them with ordure. I have heard the indians say that this animal has sometimes pulled their guns from under their heads while they were asleep, and left them so defiled."*—John Giles, *Memoirs of Odd Adventures, Strange Deliverences, & in the Captivity of John Giles, Esq.* (1736)

Wolverines are in fact not cats; they are the largest member of the mustelid family, which also includes weasels, skunks, and badgers. All members of this family have not only an oversized attitude but also pungent anal scent glands that are useful for marking territory and defense. For anyone familiar with the adaptations of the wolverine, it is easy to see why a hunter would give the animal a large dose of respect or credit it with having magical abilities. In Maine, at the southern end of its range, the wolverine was likely never very common, so it's understandable that the lumbermen, hunters, and even Henry David Thoreau had little idea of the true identity of the fearsome *lunksoos*. In fact, the wolverine was driven to extinction in Maine and neighboring Canada before the start of the twentieth century.

The language barrier probably also caused the misunderstanding of its identity. Since *lunksoos* sounds similar to the English word "lynx," this Indian Devil is most frequently misidentified as a feline predator.

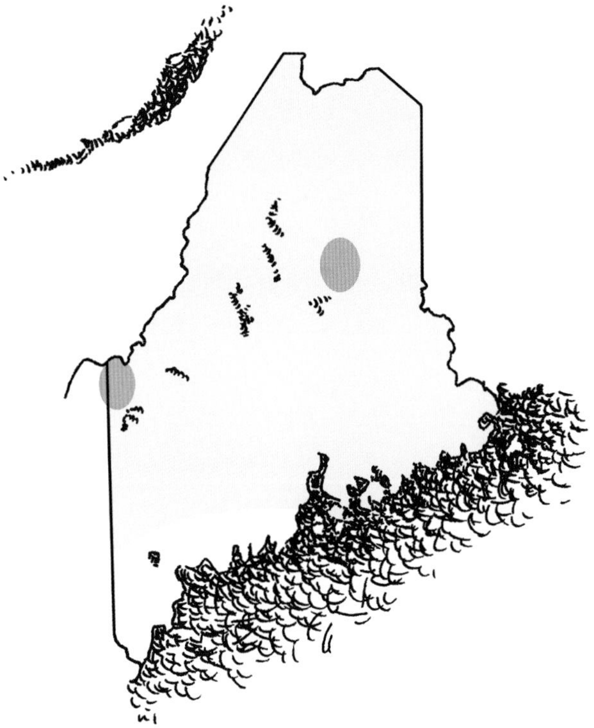

Historically the *lunksoos* was found in all but the southern sections of Maine, which lacked sufficient winter snowpack to support it. The last confirmed report of a wolverine in Maine was in the late 1800s along the northern portion of the New Hampshire border (left highlight). Today many places in and around the Katahdin Woods and Waters National Monument (right highlight) are named after the *lunksoos*.

The truth, however, can be found in old Wabanaki stories featuring an important character who was a wolverine named *Lux* (or *Laks* or *Lox*), a bad-tempered, gluttonous trickster wizard who kills for fun. In Wabanaki languages, the suffix *-sis* means "small" (much like the English *-ette*, as in "kitchenette"). The old Wabanaki term for the wolverine was *laksis*, which to the English-speaking ear sounds like *lunksoos*. Lumbermen and Thoreau variously wrote the name as "lunk soos," "lunksoos," "lunxus," "lunkson," and even "linkumsluice." No matter what the name, unfortunately, today the only *lunksoos* you are likely to encounter in Maine are the mountains, lakes, streams, and camps that bear its name. Nearly all of these are in and around the Katahdin Woods and Waters National Monument. So if you're in search of a *lunksoos*, that's a likely place to start. However, if you go there, you might need to know that these places all use a French Canadian pronunciation of the word, so it sounds more like *loonk-sew* than the original Wabanaki word.

> *"I cannot say I am terribly sad that the wolverine (or lunksoos, as the Indians call it) was killed off around these parts. By all accounts he was quite a fearless beast who would walk into camp hissing and snarling and rob you blind."*
>
> —Burton Marlborough Packard, 1892

# MERMAIDS

## Old World and Wabanaki Creatures

This hand-colored German map of North America from the early eighteenth century depicts mermaids in the North Atlantic.

**MERMAIDS ARE** people of the ocean who have the top half of a human and are fish-like from the waist down. There is a long history of accounts of various mermaids in Maine waters. In the mid-1600s, fishermen frequently saw and sometimes attempted to capture mermaids and mermen throughout Canadian and New England waters. In Maine, notable reports exist from near Mount Desert Island and in Casco Bay. In

1639, Michael Mitton, the constable of Falmouth, related an experience he had with a merman while bird hunting in Casco Bay. As he rounded a small island in his canoe, the merman put both of its human-like hands on the side of Mitton's canoe. Fearing the canoe would tip, Mitton grabbed a hatchet and cut one of the merman's hands off. Likely dying, it let go and sank into the sea, trailing a cloud of purple blood behind it.

Aside from the fleeting glimpses of European seamen and settlers, the Wabanaki have long known about mermaids and mermen in the waters off Maine. There seem to be at least two different species living along these coasts. One is aggressive and human sized, and the other is harmless to humans and only about three feet long. The two are bitter enemies and are never found together. An old story describes a great battle between them that occurred at Reversing Falls in Cobscook Bay. Farther up the coast, in Canada, the Micmac call a third species of mermaids *sabawaelnu*, or "halfway people." This is a human-sized mermaid who does no harm if treated with respect. It is said that their singing can call powerful storms.

> *"When I was a boy in Searsport, I'd always hear the sailors and sea captains talking to my father about mermaids. Many days I'd run down to the ocean hoping to see one. But now that I'm here in Willimantic I don't suppose I ever will."*
>
> —Burton Marlborough Packard, 1919

## Lumpeguin

### Wabanaki Creature

The *lumpeguin* (or *alambaguenosisak* in Penobscot) are much smaller and less sinister mermaids than the *nodumkanwet*. But these dark little people are

no less powerful in their own way. *Lumpeguin* are shape changers and frequently leave the water in the form of a small human. They also have the ability to increase their size to that of a large man or to shrink small enough to hide in a curled leaf.

Sometimes taking human form, *lumpeguin* can occasionally be seen frolicking in the waves near the shore. Don't let their size fool you—their powerful magic makes them worthy of respect.

These water spirits are often found in the sea, but they frequently venture up into rivers and may be found in deep lakes. While typically deep-water creatures, groups of them can often be seen frolicking in the waves near shore. When they play in the waves, they remove their clothes and place them on the shore (which may seem a bit strange for water spirits, but it is their way). Anyone who steals a *lumpeguin*'s clothes will have power over them. In the old days, young Wabanaki men sometimes married *lumpeguin* women whose clothes they had stolen. It's easy to understand why someone would want a *lumpeguin* wife, as they have the ability to turn a tiny piece of food into a huge feast and bake bread from snow, and any pot they cook in will produce an endless supply of food. And if marriage isn't what you are looking for, they have also been known to grant wishes to those who capture or rescue them.

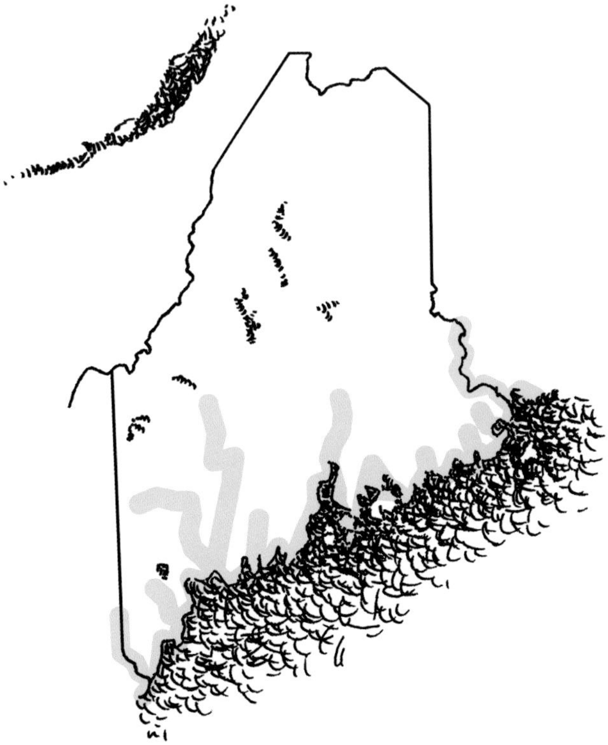

*Lumpeguin* can be found along the region's coastlines, in bays, and even in large tidal rivers.

## *Nodumkanwet*

### Wabanaki Creature

The larger mermaid species, known as *nodumkanwet* in Penobscot (or *apodumken* in Passamaquoddy), is a solitary creature of Maine's many bays and large rivers. They have short, wide faces and very long black or red hair. Their lower half is a long, serpent-like tail rather than that of a fish. Their hands are hairy and have claws. They have a dark intelligence and typically mean trouble for anyone they encounter. *Nodumkanwet* cast evil spells on those they see walking along riverbanks. They also delight in grabbing people from beneath the water, often in inappropriate places. And they steal and eat children who will not get out of the water or who go too near the shore when no one is looking.

*Nodumkanwet* are attracted to misfortune, and if they find a body in the water, they plug the mouth, nose, and eyes full of mud. One is said to live under Indian Island and was a common sight in the Penobscot River near Bangor during the 1849 cholera epidemic. Fortunately, it is said there are only twelve of these creatures. In Passamaquoddy Bay, where they are known as *apodumken*, they take the form of a giant fanged serpent. These large sea kings reportedly have the power to command sea animals such as lobster, clams, flounder, and seals. By some accounts, they are also the kings of a race of river elves known as the *manogamasak*. Once a year the twelve *nodumkanwet* gather together to devour the children they have stolen. When they get together,

Attracted to misfortune, these cruel mermaids are the bitter enemies of both humans and the *lumpeguin*. They can even take the form of a fanged sea serpent.

it is on a mountain where they transform into giant humans, dress in rich people's clothing, and make evil plans for the world. If there were more than twelve of them, the world would certainly be in real trouble.

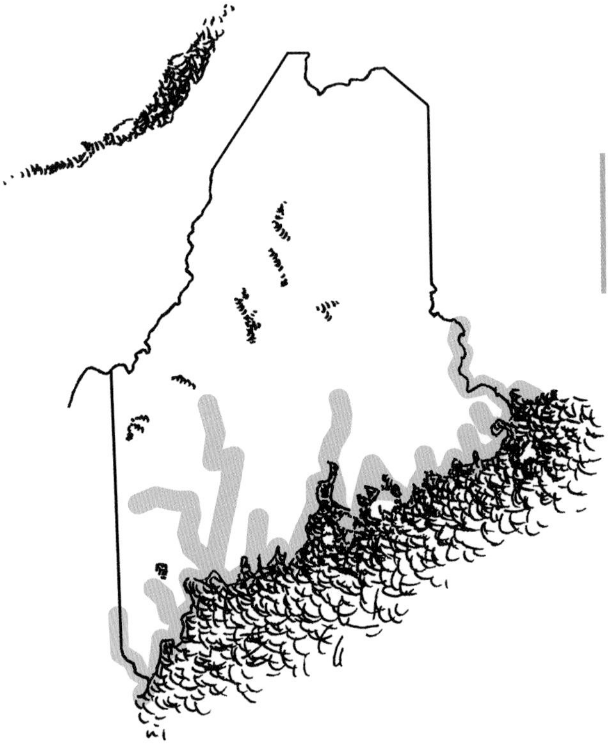

*Nodumkanwet* can be found along the region's coastlines, in bays, and even up into tidal rivers.

# MOUNTAIN LION

**Cryptid Creature**
(*Felis concolor couguar*)

> Despite being designated as extinct in Maine, hundreds of mountain lion sightings are reported each year throughout the region.

**ONCE FOUND** across the lower forty-eight states and southern Canada, North America's largest cat is also known as the cougar, panther, puma, catamount, and ghost cat. Officially, there are no longer mountain lions living in or around Maine. However, hundreds of reports are made each year about evidence of their presence. Many people believe that a population of mountain lions has persisted in the area. These large cats stand nearly three feet tall at the shoulder and can weigh up to two hundred pounds. They can measure up to eight feet in length from their nose to the tip of their long tail. Cougars have small round heads, blue eyes, and long, slender, heavily muscled bodies. Their fur can range from tawny to grayish brown in color, with lighter fur on the belly. Unlike other big cats, they lack the larynx anatomy to roar and rarely vocalize.

Powerful and stealthy, mountain lions are North America's ultimate predators. They are capable of climbing trees and even telephone poles, swimming long distances, and leaping twenty feet vertically and forty feet horizontally. With a walking speed of ten miles an hour, each animal maintains a territory of twenty-five square miles. They are secretive and prefer wild areas. Most of their diet is deer and moose. While they can sprint up to fifty miles per hour, cougars typically use a stalk and ambush strategy when hunting to avoid being injured by the hooves or antlers of their prey. This process involves leaping from cover or a tree onto their prey's back, where they grip tightly with their claws while biting through the spine or skull. Each mountain lion consumes a white-tailed deer every seven to fourteen days. In the western United States, where mountain lions are common, they have been known to attack livestock, pets, and even humans. In the past one hundred years, there have been 120 documented mountain lion attacks on humans. It's no wonder that the mountain lion has always inspired fear and wary attention.

Mountain lions once lived in every habitat across the United States, Mexico, and southern Canada, but today there are officially only breeding populations in the mountains of the western United States and in Florida. The decimation of the eastern cougar was due mostly to relentless hunting spurred on by government-funded anti-predator bounties and the near elimination of the white-tailed deer due to overhunting in the 1800s. Historically, the last cougar in the region was killed near the Quebec border of Maine in 1938. However, even by the mid-1800s, the cougar was exceedingly rare in the region. This fact is exemplified in a 1901 article for *Field and Stream* written by Manly Hardy. The respected Bangor-area naturalist and outdoorsman wrote that while he often read and heard about hunters and trappers taking cougars, he had doubts about those tales:

> I will say that though my father and myself were buyers of fur for more than seventy-five years, neither of us ever saw the skin of one of these animals taken either in Maine, New Brunswick, Nova Scotia, or Canada East. I have handled nearly or quite half a million dollars' worth of fur taken in the above places, but I have yet to hear of a single skin being taken. The same is true of the wolverene [*sic*] or carcarjou, commonly called Indian Devil, or lunksoos.

Since the eastern cougar was listed as a federally endangered species in 1973, the U.S. Fish and Wildlife Service has, like Manly Hardy, searched for conclusive proof of their occurrence. However, after decades of searching with nothing to show for it, the eastern cougar was delisted and officially declared extinct in January 2018. However, this announcement has not stopped the flow of mountain lion reports in Maine and the surrounding areas. Many people who are quite familiar with the woods and wildlife of Maine believe that a small remnant population of eastern cougars still exists in the undeveloped portions of the state. Even some game wardens and state wildlife biologists believe they have seen mountain lions. Reports of cougars occur not just in the wilder parts of northwestern Maine but throughout the state in agricultural, suburban, and even urban areas. In addition to sightings, many of these reports are based on footprints, trail and surveillance photographs, calls, hair, scat, and other secondary evidence. In a brief email interview, Dr. Walter Jakubas, the lead scientist who investigates cougar reports for the Maine Department of Inland Fish and Wildlife, described how easy it is to misidentify these types of evidence even for experienced investigators. With modern DNA analysis, it has become much easier to verify the origins of hair and scat. Some specimens formerly "confirmed" to be from mountain lions are now known to be from other animals, such as foxes, dogs, or bobcats. A 1984 article by Robert Downing, a U.S. Fish and Wildlife scientist at the Denver Research Center, echoed many of the sentiments of Dr. Jakus: "Prints can melt out, hair is nearly impossible to conclusively identify, and importantly, large bobcats often look, hunt, and leave signs nearly indistinguishable from cougars."

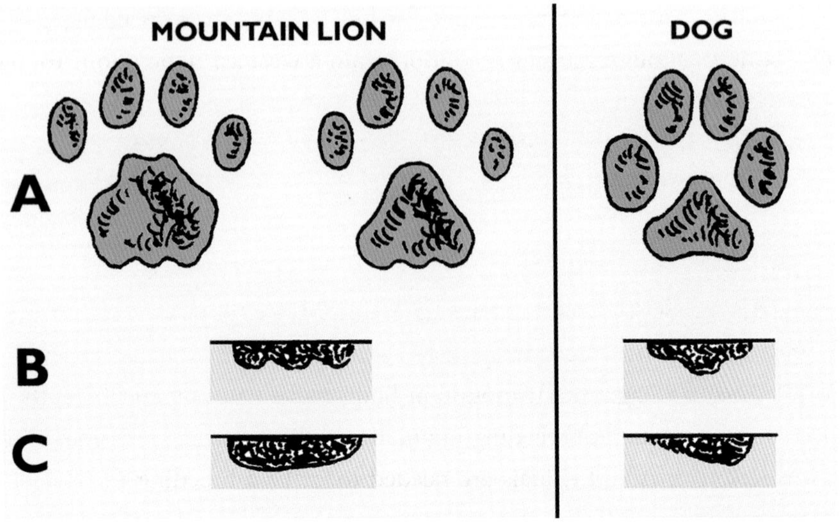


Mountain lion tracks typically exceed three inches and have a stride of over twenty-four inches, which is larger than other wildcats in the area. Large dog tracks are those most frequently confused with those of mountain lions; the presence or absence of claws is an unreliable indicator of species. Note in row A, in the mountain lion tracks, the front and rear tracks are distinct, and toe pads are widely spaced, not symmetrical, and much smaller relative to the heel pads. The heel pads also have three lobes on the rear side, compared to a dog's rounded or flat rear side of the heel pad. Row B shows the side-to-side cross section of the heel pads; note the even depth on the cougar and the dipped center in the canine. Row C shows the front-to-back cross section of the heel pads; note the strong forward slope of the dog's heel pad, compared to the cougar's level or rear slope.

Despite the difficulty of proper identification, according to the U.S. Fish and Wildlife Service, from 1900 to 2010 there have been some 108 reports east of the Mississippi with a "high likelihood of being a cougar." According to most wildlife agencies, the most likely suspect when there is a mountain lion sighting is a released domestic animal. Even though it is illegal, people can and do keep mountain lions as pets, and sometimes they get released or escape into the wild. These animals have distinctive digestive parasites, are often declawed and/or fixed, and frequently have DNA with genetic markers indicating a South American origin. In other words, there are certainly sometimes mountain lions seen in the region; however, they are likely animals that have escaped from captivity.

Another interesting possibility for how mountain lions could come to Maine is through natural migration from a western population. Young male cougars frequently travel great distances when they reach adolescence in search of their own territory and mates. Science seems to have conclusively recorded this happening. On June 11, 2011, a 140-pound male mountain lion was killed by a car on Wilbur Cross Parkway in Greenwich, Connecticut. DNA and forensic analysis showed that it was from a wild population in South Dakota, some 1,500 miles away. If a cougar could reach Connecticut, it could certainly also reach other parts of the Northeast. While scientists agree that mountain lions could naturally get here, they don't think a sustained breeding population will occur here anytime soon, since around fifty individuals are needed to make a breeding population. Additionally, unlike young males, which naturally travel long distances,

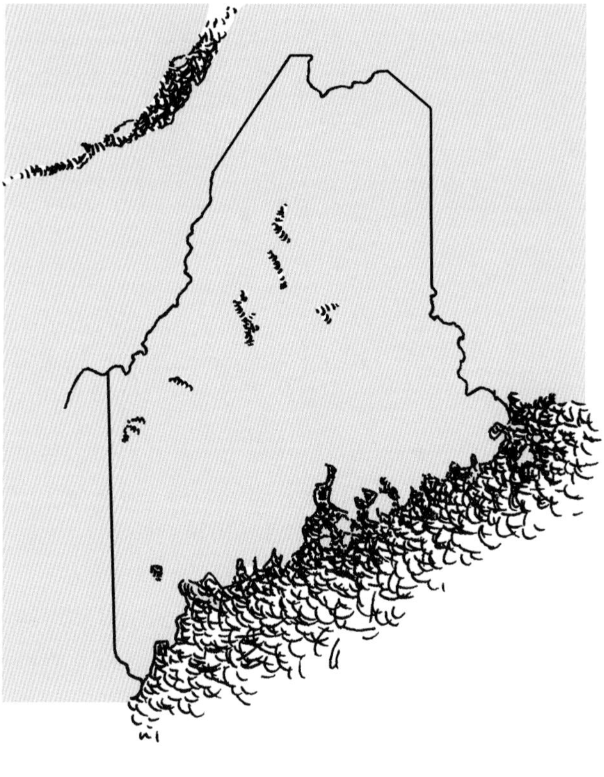

Mountain lions once roamed all of North America, and some may still be found throughout their historic range.

females typically disperse less than one hundred miles when establishing their own territory. But with three possibilities for cougars in Maine—a small native relic population leftover, a few released pets, and some new migrants—who's to say there isn't a population of cougars here already? There certainly are enough sightings each year to indicate this is likely the case. Interestingly, now that the eastern cougar has been declared extinct, it is no longer protected by the federal Endangered Species Act, meaning that it is now legal for states or Native American nations to reintroduce cougars to the area if they choose.

> *"Cryptozoologists working on other problems should thus take heart that the eastern cougar has not yet been proven to exist: it adds weight to their own cases by demonstrating, despite all arguments to the contrary, that it is very difficult to locate rare, elusive animals in wilderness areas."*
> —Robert Downing, U.S. Fish and Wildlife Service (*Cryptozoology*, 1984)

# PAMOLA

## Wabanaki Creature

**PAMOLA (OR *B'MOLE'*)** is a giant winged creature that lives on Katahdin, where one of the peaks bears his name. Pamola was so feared by the Wabanaki that they never climbed the summit of Katahdin for fear of being killed or carried off to *Alomkik*, the land of darkness. For this reason, it wasn't until 1804 that

Pamola is a giant winged being who lives atop Katahdin. For centuries he kept people off the mountain. This powerful creature should be treated with respect.

Charles Turner Jr. and his Wabanaki guides made the first recorded summit of the mountain. The Wabanaki members of the party told Turner that Pamola "inhabits [Katahdin] at least in winter, and flies off in the spring with tremendous rumbling noises." Pamola is responsible for creating the howling, swirling winds that make Katahdin a formidable mountain.

Pamola is not always harmful, though. The Wawenock Abenaki to the south tell that on the day he flies from his mountain, he crosses all Wabanaki land and will give aid to those who call him by name or signal him with smoke. Like many of the Wabanaki creatures, Pamola seems capable of changing shape—descriptions of him vary considerably. Most agree that he is a giant flying bird creature. One of the earliest accounts says Pamola's "head and face is like a man's, and his body, shape, and feet like an eagle, and that he can take up a moose with one of his claws." Another early account describes Pamola as having a huge head but almost no body, a horrible beak and talons, and gigantic wings that drag on the ground. This second account is attributed to Governor John Neptune and later his granddaughter, Clara Neptune.

Another Wabanaki creature, the *chebelaque* (or *tci'pilakw* or *geebellowk*), has a very similar description to Pamola and may be the same creature. This "spirit of the night air" is all head and heart with long legs, large talons, and giant wings. Its large eyes can sometimes be seen grinning down from the crotch of trees. When a *chebelaque* attacks, it screeches and resembles a diving owl; nothing can harm it, and whoever it attacks is doomed.

The only early Wabanaki sketch of Pamola was done by Penobscot chief Arexes in 1775. In it a huge winged head with an enormous eye can be seen carrying away a human in its long talons.

Perhaps the best-known account of Pamola is Leroy Dudley's friendlier but still formidable version of Pamola

described in the book *Chimney Pond Tales*. Dudley was a famous Katahdin guide of the early twentieth century who told many stories of his encounters with Pamola. Dudley described him this way: "He stood eighteen or twenty feet tall, with body and legs like a man, but all covered with coarse hair like a moose. His head was like a moose and his ears and horns, but he had kind of a big curved beak like an eagle. He had a great long beard on his chin, as much as three feet long or longer." He goes on to describe Pamola as having bat wings and glowing eyes. Dudley's version of Pamola is the familiar one used on logos and scout badges. Some early accounts mistakenly connect the name Pamola to various other dangerous creatures, such as big cats or even cannibal giants, but Pamola is certainly a winged creature.

This early sketch of Pamola by Father Eugene Ventromile (1884) confuses Pamola with a Wabanaki giant, but it does capture the lack of a body except for a heart.

From its founding in 2010 until 2017, the Lewiston-based Baxter Brewing Company used a logo featuring a version of Leroy Dudley's moose-headed Pamola on nearly all its products.

There are some large caves in the Northwest Basin of Katahdin that are said to be Pamola's home. No one sees Pamola much these days; perhaps he's moved on. Or perhaps he spends more time in *Alomkik* now that his friend Mr. Dudley is gone. But if you go up Katahdin and you run into Pamola, be brave and treat him with respect, for that's the only way that anyone has ever survived an encounter with him.

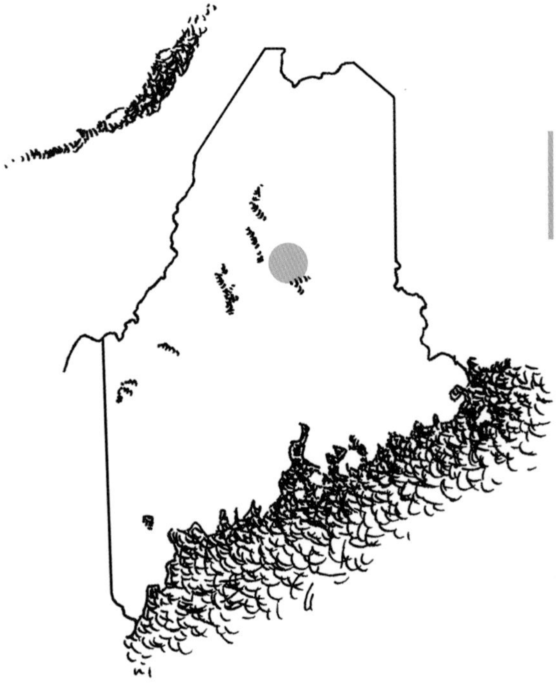

Pamola's home is on Maine's tallest mountain, Katahdin.

# SEA SERPENT

## Old World and Cryptid Creature

*(Plurigibbosus novae-angliae)*

**THE SEAS** from Boston to Nova Scotia were once a hotbed of sea serpent sightings. While rarely sighted today, New England's sea serpent is easily the best-attested sea monster in the world. Since the first record in 1639, more than two hundred sightings have been recorded by knowledgeable and reliable

Hundreds of sea serpent sightings have been recorded in the Gulf of Maine. These giant serpents are impressive but seem to be largely harmless.

people, including sea captains, fishermen, ministers, lawyers, and businesspeople. The creature's most frequent appearances have been off Cape Ann, Massachusetts, but nearly as many sightings have been from Maine, especially in and around Casco and Penobscot Bays. In Portland's Casco Bay, the serpent is affectionately known by the nickname Cassie.

Witnesses describe the sea serpent as a 30- to 150-foot-long snake-like creature with a black or brown back and lighter belly. It has a habit of lying motionless on the surface, where its humped back is reported to resemble barrels, buoys, or garbage bags. When moving, it can travel at surprisingly fast speeds. Its movement is almost always reported to have a unique up-and-down, corkscrewing, or serpentine undulation to its body. Indeed, this unmistakable movement is like that of no other creature, except perhaps a leech. Unlike a leech, however, while swimming the serpent holds it head several feet above the water on a long neck. Its head is large and snake- or horse-like, and it is sometimes reported to have frills or horns but usually not. Likewise, fins are occasionally reported on the body and tail but usually not. Its skin is described variously as loose, scaly, or smooth. However, one thing witnesses agree on is that it could definitely not be mistaken for any familiar animal.

An 1886 illustration of the New England sea serpent in front of Egg Rock off Lynn, Massachusetts.

It might seem troubling that not all descriptions of the serpent are alike in details, but, as every lawyer and police officer knows, it's quite normal for eyewitness accounts of events like an accident or robbery to vary considerably between people. So, in many ways, it would be even more suspect if all the witnesses of sea serpents gave precisely the same description. Overall, there is general agreement; a typical account containing many of these details can be found in a letter from the fisherman Albert Wass of Addison, Maine, about an 1898 encounter. Wass was aboard a fishing sloop in the mouth of Frenchman Bay. The vessel turned to investigate a curious splashing and the circular motion of an object protruding from the water near a large black mass. Upon closer inspection, the sight went from curious to extraordinary. The letter, in part, reads:

> At first we thought it must be a whale being attacked by a thrasher or swordfish, but on nearer approach, we were convinced that it was something different from what we had ever encountered. When we had reached a proximity of about 100 yards (and, believe me that was close enough!), the monster straightened itself out to a form resembling a seventy-five-foot string of hogsheads. Whether the body was creased in section or the coloring camouflaged it as such, I'm not sure. It carried its head, which was like that of a horse, six feet higher than its body, the motion of its swimming was like an eel, and its speed at least 20 knots. The absence of fins and the eel-like shape of the tail settled all doubt that this could be any type of whale.

While sea serpents seem curious about ships and human activity, they have almost never been recorded attacking. They are frequently seen moving their heads to look at the world above the surface. This behavior and some additional details are seen in a 1905 account by retired Major General Henry C. Merriam, a native of Houlton, Maine. He wrote in a letter to the United States National Museum about his encounter with a sea serpent near Wood Island Light, Maine. His account is quite striking, and as a long-serving and distinguished army commander, inventor of the framed canvas infantry backpack, and Medal of Honor recipient, the character of the witness couldn't be more reliable.

> We were startled by a loud splashing in the water some distance off our stern and were looking in that direction [when] we saw what appeared to be a monster serpent. Its head was several feet above the surface of the water, its body was plainly visible, slowly moving toward our boat by a sinuous or snake-like motion. . . . The animal continued its course, passing entirely around our boat . . . keeping a distance of about three hundred yards. It swam at a steady and rapid rate, not less than 12 miles an hour, keeping its head uniformly about four feet out of the water and apparently intent upon examining our craft on all sides. It had no dorsal fin, unless it was continuous.
>
> The color of its back appeared to be brown and mottled, shading down to a dull yellow on its belly. The head was like that of a snake, and that part shown above the surface—that is, the neck—appeared to be about fifteen or eighteen inches in diameter. I estimate its length at sixty feet or more. During all the time occupied in swimming around us, which must have been at least ten minutes, the head remained uniformly above the surface of the water and then it quietly dove and disappeared.

Interestingly, serpents have most frequently been seen in the summer, from June to August. This is also the time of the year in which schools of mackerel, pollock, and herring come into bays to spawn. Many believe that serpents frequent near-shore areas at this time because they are following their food. Sightings have declined sharply since the 1930s, with some believing that sea serpents have become another victim of overfishing in the Gulf of Maine. Perhaps there are no longer enough fish to sustain them, or perhaps entanglement in fishing gear has decimated their numbers as it has sea turtles and many species of marine mammals. Another theory is that the creature's absence is due to its dislike of motorized boats, causing it to avoid areas with frequent boat traffic, which has certainly become more frequent since the 1930s.

Skeptics may argue that there is too much variety in descriptions of the creature for it to be real. However, some believe that there may actually be

Sea serpents have frequently been sighted in waters along the coast from Boston to Nova Scotia.

two different types of sea creatures. According to Loren Coleman, world-famous Maine cryptozoologist, the other type of sea monster that is found in the Gulf of Maine is a water horse. Like the snake-like serpent, the water horse is a long-necked creature with a large head also shaped like that of a horse. Unlike the serpent, however, the water horse would appear to have only a single hump behind the neck, much the way an extinct plesiosaur might appear. Water horses have four flippers and sometimes venture into freshwater or even onto land. Their tracks have been sighted up to one hundred feet out of the water. They have mostly been sighted around Mount Desert Island and in Penobscot Bay. In 1819, the skeleton of one of these creatures was said to have been found washed up on Great Cranberry Island, near Mount Desert Island.

It is also worth noting that two Wabanaki creatures might fit the description of the more familiar sea serpents. Not only are there stories, but petroglyphs can also be found throughout Maine. The Wabanaki's *weewill-mekq* is a giant horned serpent or worm with a horse-shaped head that lives in both salt and freshwater. And the Passamaquoddy have legends of the *apodumken* in Passamaquoddy and Machias Bays. It is a large fanged sea serpent that, like a mermaid, sometimes has the face or body of a woman.

> *"As a boy I went sailing on a ship my father built, and the captain told me he'd seen a sea serpent just down the bay. The whole trip I kept my eye on the water hoping to see one's long neck rise above the waves."*
>
> —Burton Marlborough Packard, 1911

# SIDEHILL GOUGER

## Fearsome Critter of the Lumberwoods

(*Membriinequales declivitatis*)

**PERHAPS THE** most widely known fearsome critter of the Maine woods is the sidehill gouger. Its uneven legs on either side of its body make it perfectly adapted to living in hilly and mountainous places. Gougers keep the side of

Sidehill gougers have uneven left and right legs so they can walk around a hill and keep their back level. They are responsible for "gouging" out deep paths on hillsides.

their body with short legs on the uphill side so they can stand with a level back on steep slopes. Whenever a well-worn winding trail goes along the side of a slope rather than up it, you can be sure it is a gouger path. In fact, these shy creatures were discovered by early lumbermen due to their many deeply gouged-out winding paths. In Vermont, a variety of these animals known as *wampahoofus* is found on the slopes of Mount Mansfield. Later, farmers there crossbred them with cows so they could more easily graze on mountain sides.

While uneven legs are a great adaptation for slopes, on flat ground it causes gougers to walk in endless circles. For this reason, it was long unknown how these animals could spread from their original home in New England throughout the rest of the country. It seems that it takes gougers of two varieties, one with its long legs on the left side and the other with its long legs on the right side. A pair of gougers—one "right-handed" and one "left-handed"—can cross flat ground by leaning on one another, much as two injured soldiers might do to support each other.

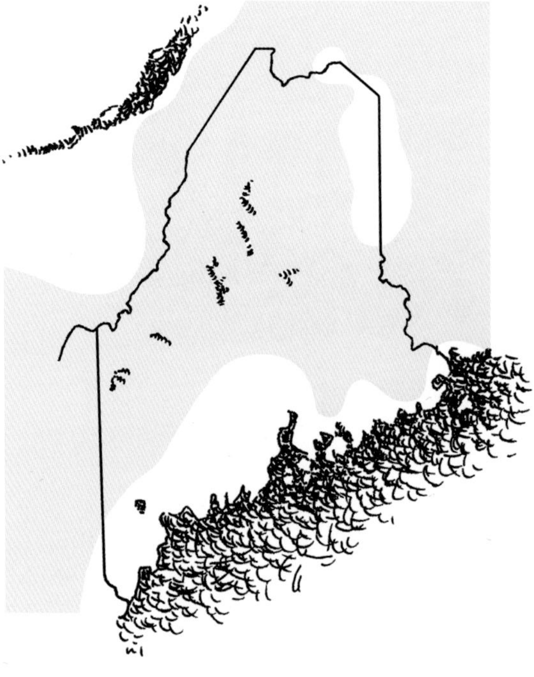

Once restricted to New England, sidehill gougers can now be found on steep hills and mountains across North America.

Gougers can be hunted by heading them off with dogs or a group of hunters. When the spooked gouger attempts to turn, it puts its longer legs uphill, causing it to tip over. Though their meat is deadly, their fat is prized for its ability to cure poisoning caused by the will-am-alone and the snow snake.

Gougers are about the size of a small deer but have a more graceful face with long, rabbit-like ears, an ample tail, and a shaggy coat. The sidehill gouger is alive and well in Maine, and I grew up following its trails, which my grandfather showed me. In most places, it is shy and almost pitiful, not dangerous. However, in Island Falls, Maine, a variety known as the sidehill dowager eats only children who have gone into the hills after dark. On each hill, there are always four dowagers, and their long gray hair rustles as they go around and around all night, looking for prey. They can run very fast, but, like most sidehill creatures, they can't go uphill or down, only around.

This widespread and fearsome critter has a variety of names, including sidehill linger, sidehill winder, sidehill doger, sidehill wowser, sidehill badger, sidewinder, gyascutus, godaphro, prock, wampus cat, and wampahoofus.

> *"If you meet a gouger coming the other way, you can give him a scare, and he'll turn and tip right over with legs flailing in the air. It's too bad gougers aren't good eating; they sure aren't hard to catch."*
>
> —Burton Marlborough Packard, 1899

# SNIPE

## Strange Bird of the Wetlands

(*Gallinago delicata*)

**THE SNIPE** hunt is one of the best-known and most widespread pranks played on unsuspecting newcomers to the forest. In the prank, snipes are described variously but always as unusual, dim-witted, and easy-to-catch birds. The newbie is then sent into a marsh or woods

Snipes are easy to catch, and hunting them is fun! Just head out to a marsh or the woods at night with a bag and make a soft whistle. Meanwhile, your friends will head in from the other direction and herd the snipe toward you. It's a sure thing.

at night with a bag or pillowcase in which to catch the snipe. Meanwhile, their companions supposedly go the other way into the forest and "flush" the snipe toward them. After the poor victim has returned from a long and "amusing" hunt with no snipe in his or her bag, they are usually told by the tricksters (who have been sitting around the fire the whole time) that there is no such bird as a snipe. But this last joke is on the trickster, because snipes are in fact very real, very strange, and very common throughout the area. *And* snipes are quite impossible to catch in a bag.

The snipe is a chubby-bodied, mid-sized brown bird of freshwater wetlands. They have several amazing adaptations. For instance, the snipe's eyes are so far back they almost literally have eyes in the backs of their heads, making it almost impossible to sneak up on one. Its long bill is flexible and has special sensory pits at the tip to help it detect buried insects and worms in the mud. Like using a straw, it slurps its prey up its bill without having to pull its bill out or even open it.

In the warm months of the breeding season, the snipe can be found throughout northern New England and Canada (green). In the winter, it migrates south, and during migration it can be found in southern New England (blue). In southern Nova Scotia and along the St. Lawrence River (pink), the snipe does not migrate and can be found year-round.

Like many birds, the snipe is migratory and can only be found in Maine during the spring, summer, and fall. During the breeding season, the males can be seen bill "jousting" to defend their territory. To attract a mate, they make a low-pitched "winnowing," which sounds like a clucking owl. This sound is not produced by singing, but rather by the bird using its wings to force air over the tail feathers. The female snipe nearly always lays four eggs. Both the male and the female snipe are excellent parents, though not in a traditional way. When the chicks hatch, the father takes the first two from the nest and the mother cares for the second two. The two parties then go their separate ways, and that is typically the last they see of each other.

> *"I don't know why, but whenever I mention that I'm going snipe hunting it gets a laugh from the sports from away. I love the first few frosts of the fall; they mean the snipes are around. An evening of walking through a wet meadow or a marsh will kick up dozens of snipes. If my wits are quick enough, I'll even be able to shoot a few. It's quite a welcome challenge."*
>
> —Burton Marlborough Packard, 1907

# SNOW SNAKE

**Fearsome Critter of the Lumberwoods**

(*Aestatesommus hiemepericulosus*)

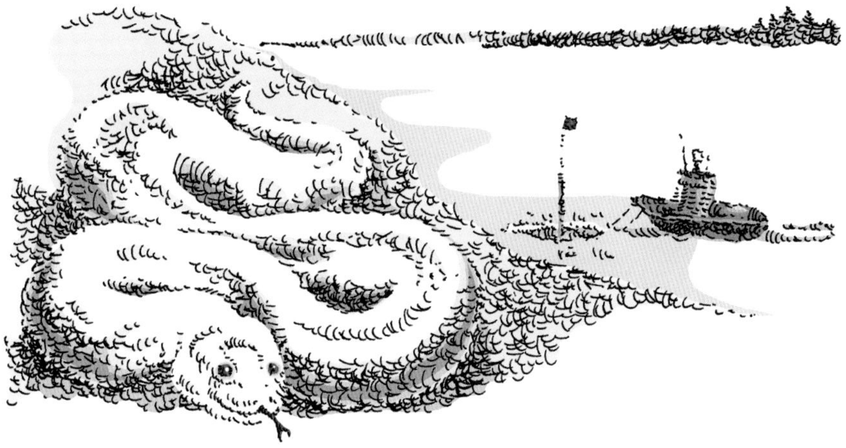

**UNLIKE MOST** snakes, the snow snake loves snow and is active in the winter while hibernating in the summer. They are entirely white except for their small red eyes, which are always kept partially closed. This characteristic allows snow snakes almost perfect camouflage as they lie in wait for partridges or snowshoe hares. Their tracks and burrows in the snow are much more frequently seen than the snake itself. Interestingly, smaller snakes often leave yellow holes and tracks in the snow.

Snow snakes can be quite deadly in the winter due to their perfect camouflage and chilling venom. Beware their yellowish burrows in the snow.

Like most snakes, they are not aggressive toward humans unless disturbed, which is good since snow snakes have very toxic venom. A bite instantly begins to chill and paralyze its prey. If an arm or leg is bitten by a snow snake, it will immediately feel cold and lose sensation, eventually turning black. Only tanglefoot oil or the fat of a sidehill gouger can save the victim. Sometimes alcoholic beverages can neutralize snow snake venom as well.

Once the winter terror of lumberjacks, these animals are now most often seen by ice fishermen, snowmobilers, and skiers. Many a fight has been caused between an ice fisherman and his spouse when the latter was trapped by an angry snow snake in his icehouse much longer than expected. In such a case, there is no choice but to keep fishing. Seasoned ice fishermen know the best time to safely see snow snakes is near ice out, when they can be seen chewing on the ice near the open water. Skiers and snowboarders, however, know these animals best from the tremendous wipeouts they cause when they coil around a ski or snowboard from beneath the snow.

A tree-dwelling variety of snow snake can also be found from the Adirondacks to Maine (*Aestatesommus hiemepericulosus* var. *arborialus*). This variety hunts by dropping down on its prey from an overhanging branch. Compared to their drift-dwelling cousins, they are more aggressive but also less deadly. They attack when an unsuspecting person passes under a

Carved wooden snow snakes, traditionally ranging 14–24 inches, are used by the Penobscot people to play a game called snow snakes. The snakes are slid down a track in the snow created by dragging a young boy down a snowy incline.

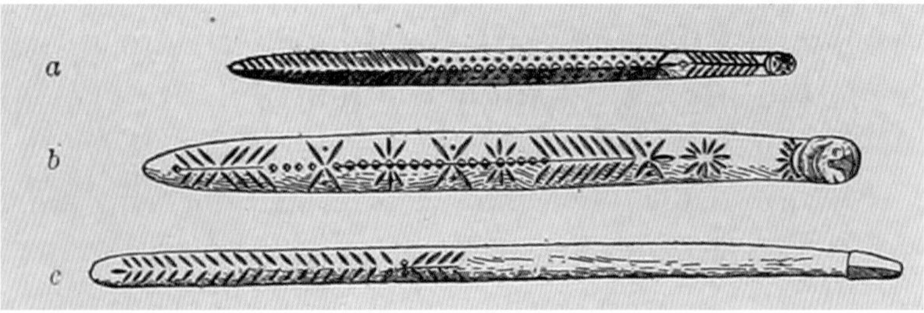

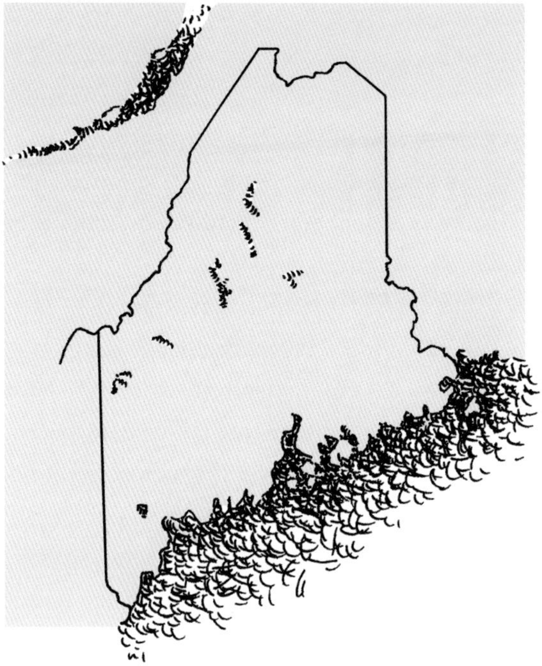

Snow snakes can be found across snowy areas of North America.

low-hanging branch with their head down. The snow snake drops down onto the exposed neck and crawls down into the victim's shirt. There they quickly disappear, leaving only a wet spot and a chilled feeling from their mildly toxic bite. Aside from being annoying and amusing to your friends, the tree-dwelling snow snake is fairly harmless.

Interestingly, Wabanaki and Algonquin people across North America play a winter game called "snow snake." In the game, long, weighted sticks that are carved into the likeness of a snake are thrown or slid down a smooth track made in the snow. The snake that goes the farthest is the winner.

> *"A snow snake is nothing to mess with. Doesn't matter if you got tanglefoot oil or not, that cold soaks into your bones for weeks."*
>
> —Burton Marlborough Packard, 1887

# SPECTER MOOSE

## Fearsome Critter of the Lumberwoods

(*Alces alces phasma*)

Specter moose are giant white moose that can aggressively command respect or simply disappear in an instant. Some say that it is the spirit of all moose.

**SPECTER MOOSE** are the great white giants of the northern forest. Other than the light color and their secretive nature, there's nothing ghostly about the fifteen-foot-tall specter moose. In fact, they can be quite aggressive, and with a ten-foot rack of antlers and weighing thousands of pounds, they are not to be taken lightly. Luckily, they are much more likely to slip away before being noticed than to attack. Some say they have an almost magical ability to disappear instantly when encountered. Others attribute their elusiveness to a keen sense of smell and excellent hearing. Either way, this vanishing act is amazing given their dusky white coloration and immense size.

The *New York Times* reported the first known sighting in 1891 by famed Lobster Lake guide Clarence Duffy. Specter moose have since been sighted throughout the region around Moosehead Lake and the 100 Mile Wilderness Area. These white giants are often seen associating with regular moose and are likely not a unique species, but rather a genetic variant within the standard moose population. These woodland giants are not albinos, however, as they do not have red eyes.

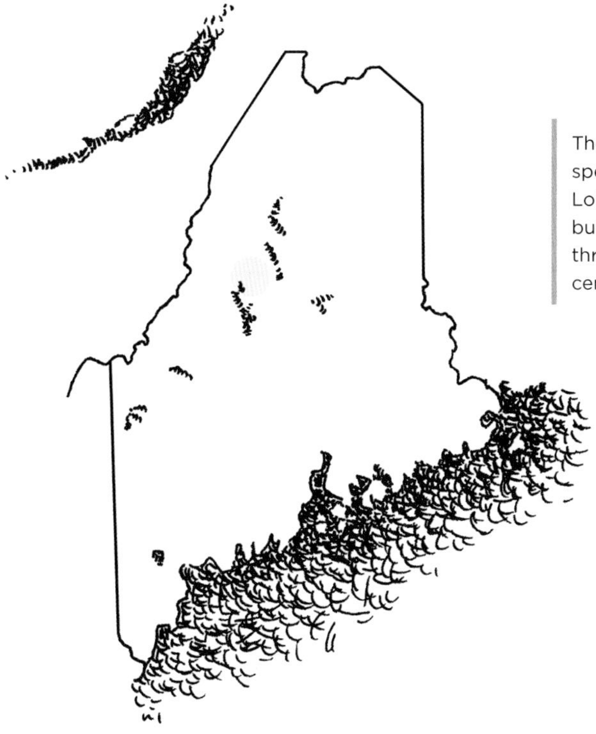

The first sighting of the specter moose was near Lobster Lake (blue), but it has been sighted throughout the forests of central and northern Maine.

Specter or ghost moose is also a term applied to moose who are heavily infested with winter ticks (*Dermacentor albipictus*). Infested moose rub themselves against trees in an attempt to remove the irritating ticks, which causes their dark guard hairs to break, leaving the coat a light dusky gray color. Winter ticks are a major parasite of moose and in bad years can cause heavy losses to the moose population. Moose sometimes carry so many of these parasites (up to 150,000 have been recorded on one animal) that it causes anemia or death. However, winter tick infections are likely not the cause of the specter moose sightings, as the ghostly coloration caused by hair loss is typically limited to only late winter and spring.

> *"After reading Duffy's account of the Great White Moose, Sam and I decided to head up to Lobster Lake to see if we could bag the fellow. We did see some unusually large tracks, but unfortunately no giant white moose's head will be hanging on the Lake House's wall."*
>
> —Burton Marlborough Packard, 1892

# TOTE ROAD SHAGAMAW

## Fearsome Critter of the Lumberwoods

(*Bipedester delusissimus*)

**THE TOTE** road shagamaw has a huge appetite for clothing, gloves, and boots. They're usually the ones responsible if these items go missing. While wool is their favorite, they will eat any clothing they find in the woods. This strange creature has four legs, but it walks on only two. It has the front legs of a bear and the back legs of a moose. They are almost impossible to track because every quarter mile or so their tracks change from moose to bear when they swing their bodies around and walk on their other set of legs. While they are large and fierce looking, they're actually shy and curious.

Shagamaws are very imitative and developed their habits from watching people in the woods. In the nineteenth and twentieth centuries, they mostly watched timber cruisers and surveyors. So it is not surprising that they follow blazed lines, have a pace that is exactly a yard long, or

These scruffy-looking creatures like to mimic and lurk as they walk down woodland roads and trails. They're harmless but always waiting for an opportunity to steal something you've left at camp.

switch legs every 440 steps. Much like surveyors, they even change direction at corner markers and witness trees.

But with the end of the logging camps and the start of today's GPS-driven lumber surveying, there has been a sharp decrease in shagamaw sightings. However, the shagamaw may be just as common as ever; perhaps they have simply started mimicking Appalachian Trail hikers. It would, after all, be hard to tell a shaggy-looking thru-hiker from a shagamaw.

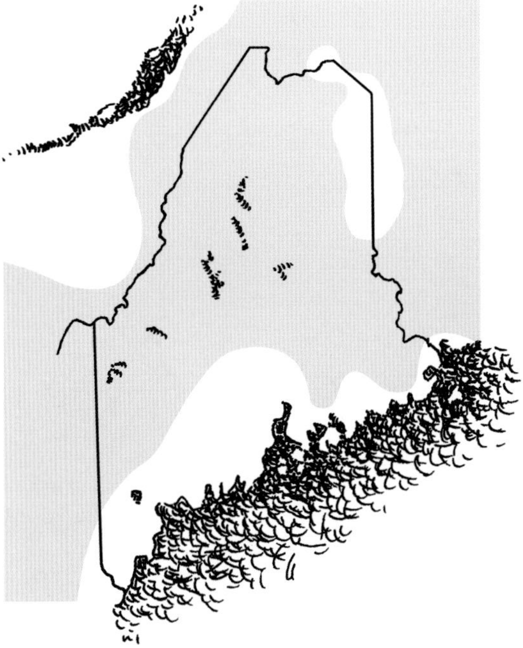

Shagamaws can be found throughout the forests of Maine.

*"When I went to sleep I hung my pants up to dry outside the camp. This morning they were gone! How is it possible that I can lose my pants in the woods?"*

—Burton Marlborough Packard, 1910

# TREE SQUEAK

**Fearsome Critter of the Lumberwoods**

(*Arborexusta stridens*)

**EVERYONE HAS** probably heard a tree squeak. But most people who hear its squeaking think it's just the sound of the trees moving in the wind. Very few people have ever seen one of

Trees don't squeak. That's the tree squeak you hear. These little creatures make a racket when the wind blows because they are helpless if they're blown off their branch.

these canopy dwellers. They are small weasel-like creatures with rough skin instead of fur. They spend most of the day motionless, wrapped around branches and waiting for a meal of insects, small birds, or rodents. They become quite active during long dry spells, when they might be seen running up and down the trees making gibbering noises and drooling. They are also quite active around dusk. But don't get too close, as these little guys are wicked and will deliver a nasty bite with their sharp teeth.

Tree squeaks are very social, and in high winds they can be heard calling to make sure the others in their group are still there. While best known for their squeaking, they make a variety of other sounds, such as low whines, creaking, and sharp cracking noises. One of the reasons tree squeaks can get around trees so well is that their legs have evolved into suction cup–like appendages. John "Jack" Dudley, of the Alexander-Crawford Historical Society in Washington County, is the only person known to

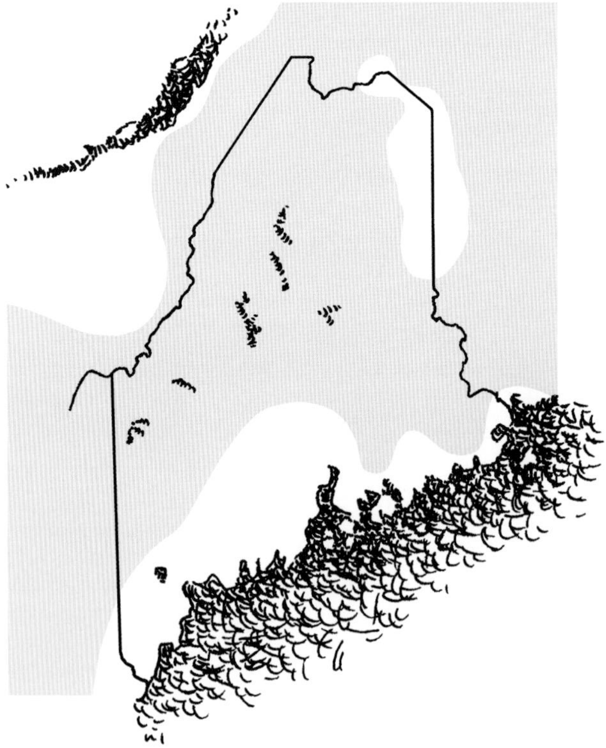

Tree squeaks can be found in woodlands across the region and beyond.

have a preserved specimen of a tree squeak. He once was given three dead tree squeaks by a Micmac friend. The wind had apparently blown them from their tree, and once on the ground they were helpless and starved to death. Unfortunately for them, because of their suction-cup limbs, they are unable to move on the ground. Usually, the only way they can move from tree to tree is along branches or other objects that allow trees to touch. However, when there's a bright moon on hot and humid summer nights, it is said they can be seen floating through the moonbeams from one tree to another.

Tree squeaks seem to prefer hardwood trees to evergreens. Because of their limited ability to move from tree to tree, logging has done a number on their population. However, while rarer than they once were, this animal is alive and well in Maine, and I grew up hearing it in the trees around the Sebec Lake region. My family always referred to them as "freshwater tree squeaks." But despite investigation, I am unsure whether those that live nearer to the saltwater coast are indeed a distinct variety.

> *"It is well known that the tree squeak is good eating, but I had no idea they could deliver such a nasty bite."*
>
> —Burton Marlborough Packard, 1884

# TURNER BEAST

## Cryptid Creature

One thing is for sure—the Turner beast is not a dog. This mysterious creature has been terrorizing people and attacking animals in the area around Lewiston since at least the 1990s.

**SINCE AT** least the mid-1990s, residents across central Maine have reported a "mystery beast" lurking in the woods and countryside. The canine creature has been blamed for killing dogs, cats, and sheep and for spooking people. The large creature has been described as a mutant dog or wolf-hybrid with a short muzzle and high front shoulders like a hyena. Witnesses agree that it has enormous eyes, a large head, dark ragged fur, and a noticeably foul stench. It has little fear of people and often investigates buildings and stares people down.

Most of the sightings have centered around the Lewiston-Auburn area of Androscoggin and Kennebec Counties. This so-called mutant beast has been blamed for killing a Doberman and mauling a Rottweiler. In 2006, a large canine matching the description was killed by a car on Route 4 in Turner, which brought nationwide media attention to the area. Reporters have since dubbed this creature the Turner beast. DNA testing later determined the body was an ordinary dog. In 2007, the cable television show *Monster Quest* featured the creature in an episode called "Mutant Canines." The show and other sources have speculated that it may be the same type of creature as Montana's Shunka Warakin or Ringdocus, which witnesses describe similarly to Maine's mystery beast. This creature and others like it are sometimes thought to be an Ice Age dire wolf (*Canis dirus*). Another hypothesis is that Maine's mystery beast may be a dark-colored gray wolf (*Canis lupus*), a species that used to live in Maine but now only ranges here occasionally from Canada, where the nearest breeding population is only seventy-five miles away in Quebec.

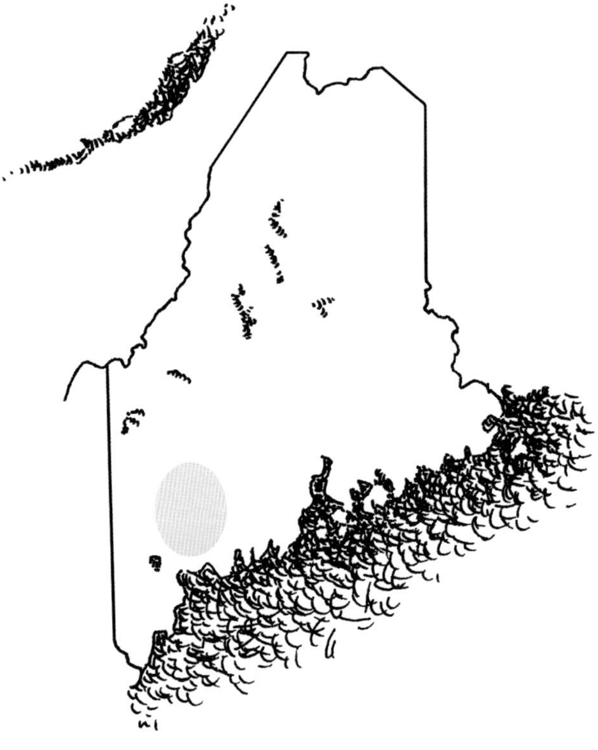

The Turner beast has been sighted across Androscoggin County around the towns of Lewiston, Auburn, Litchfield, Sabattus, Leeds, Greene, New Gloucester, Wales, Wayne, Auburn, and Turner.

It's hard to ignore the similarity between a dark or black canine with no fear of humans and the French-Canadian legends of the *loup garou*, but that werewolf is a dark sorcerer who can change shape from human to a larger, otherworldly wolf-like creature. Other locals who have heard of the Turner beast also have theories that it might be a bear, the Indian Devil *lunksoos*, or even an alien creature.

Or perhaps this creature is an Old World immigrant, as the description matches almost exactly with a creature from Europe called the hellhound. In the British Isles, there are legends of hellhounds, such as the Barghest or Black Shuck, which are said to be the inspiration for the Sherlock Holmes novel *The Hound of the Baskervilles*. Interestingly, there are historic reports of similar terrorizing fairy hounds in New Brunswick and Nova Scotia. But in all places, these powerful creatures are both ghostly and physical. In some European legends, they join the wild hunt; in others, they guard lonely forests, roadways, or cemeteries. Details may vary, but meeting the large-eyed gaze of a hellhound is always terrifying and often foretells misfortune or death.

Helloound, *loup garou*, wolf, dog, or something else? We might not know what exactly the Androscoggin mystery beast is, but we can be certain something is out there.

> *"It's got some extra claws that I find interesting. They're sticking up like horns of a devil. I'll be looking into that."*—Loren Coleman, crytozoologist (*Lewiston Sun Journal*, 2006)

### ***Gray Wolf in Maine***

In 2017, the gray wolf (*Canis lupus*) was officially removed from the endangered species list and declared extinct in Maine when the U.S. Fish and Wildlife Service announced that there was no evidence of a breeding population here. However, wolves were once so common and problematic that bounties were paid to wolf hunters until 1903. By that time, the deer, caribou, beaver, and moose populations on which wolves depend were so depleted that wolves probably would not have survived. Wolves may someday make a comeback in Maine—the nearest breeding population is in Quebec, only seventy-five miles from the Maine border. Young wolves leave their pack and frequently travel great distances, sometimes as far as five hundred miles, in search of new territories. In fact, two wolves were killed in Maine as recently as 1993 and 1996. It is also interesting to note that the coyote population in Maine has been found to carry a large number of wolf genes from interbreeding with wolves. As a result, coyotes in the Northeast are ten pounds larger and behave in ways more like wolves than those found in the western United States.

# WAMFAHOOFUS

## Fearsome Critter of the Lumberwoods

(*Limmertakus boottii*)

This little boot-grabbing puddle dweller was first discovered in the White Mountains by Dr. Francis Boott in the 1800s.

**WHEN HIKING,** always stay to the left of any puddles or boggy areas that you encounter, or the one-armed wamfahoofus may grab your boot. These curious creatures have a voracious appetite for boot leather, and they're not too shy to reach out and grab your feet. Often all that can be seen of a lurking wamfahoofus is its single bubble-shaped eye that sticks up out of mucky water. The rest of the body is rather like a leathery lily pad that floats just below the surface and anchors itself deep in the muck, where it can quickly withdraw itself if threatened. Since it only has a right arm, anyone unlucky enough to step near a wamfahoofus's right side while walking through a puddle will find it grabs on tight. And while these animals prefer to eat only boot leather, they'll take any footwear they can get. For their small size, they are very strong and often come away with shoes. If you are successful in rescuing your footwear, you will likely hear a sad "*schckckckklooop*" sound, which is the cry of a hungry wamfahoofus.

I've found these creatures can sometimes be pulled from the muck by probing them with a specially made wamfahoofus-rod. This tool is much like a ladle handle, a flat piece of metal about eighteen inches long with a curved hook on the end. This hook is used to grab them under the arm and pull them from the mud.

First known by part of its scientific name, *Limmertakus boottii*, this animal was discovered by Dr. Francis Boott (1792–1863), a famous

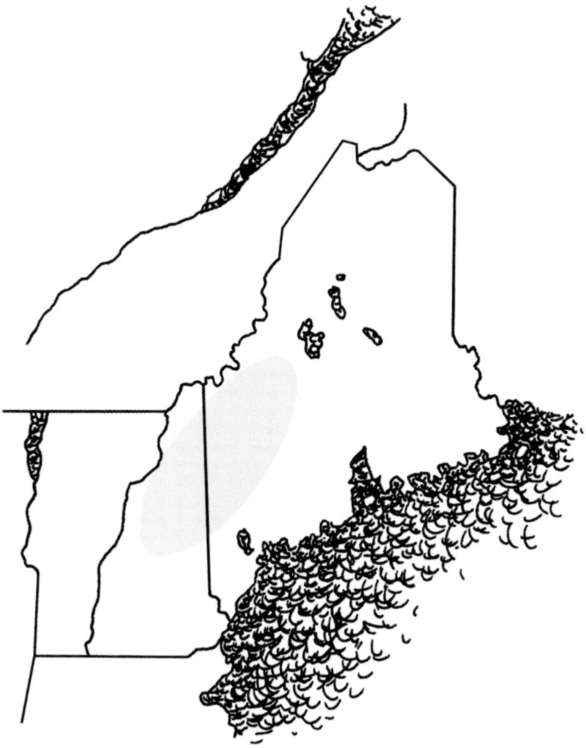

The wamfahoofus can be found throughout the White Mountains of New Hampshire and Maine.

naturalist of the White Mountains. Both this fearsome critter and a minor peak southeast of Mount Washington now bear Dr. Boott's name. The first full modern scientific account of this creature seems to have been recorded by A. J. Oxton. The common name, *wamfahoofus*, seems to be inspired in some way by the sound heard when children stomp in trail mud.

> *"Darn mud puddle got my boot. It was almost like something grabbed ahold of it and wouldn't let go until the boot was off. Never did find it."*
>
> —Burton Marlborough Packard, 1920

# WEDGE-LEDGE CHOMPER

## Fearsome Critter of the Lumberwoods

(*Saxea comedentis*)

**IF YOU** are hiking on a rocky slope and see a recently broken rock or a new rockslide, it's likely the work of a wedge-ledge chomper. This hippopotamus-size creature scrapes away stone ledges and breaks up rocks with its enormous bulldozer-like mouth. They seem to

These slow-moving and secretive giants are responsible for rockslides and mountain erosion. They can be as large as a car or as small as a football, but they are rarely seen due to their perfect camouflage.

enjoy carving out tiers or step-like structures in rock ledges and hillsides. Once the rocks are broken, the chompers eat the pieces they can fit in their mouths. It's unclear what they get out of the rocks because they seem to come out just the same as they went in. Chompers rarely venture far and usually return to the same place each night to feed.

Despite their size and slow-moving natures, they are rarely noticed. Most people mistake them for boulders, which is easy to do since their skin looks just like the stones around them—some even have moss and lichen growing on their backs. Wedge-ledge chompers have excellent hearing and are quite shy, so when they notice someone coming, they just hunch over and wait motionlessly, like a rock, for the human to pass by. It takes a keen observer to notice that a boulder is not in exactly the same place it was the last time they came by.

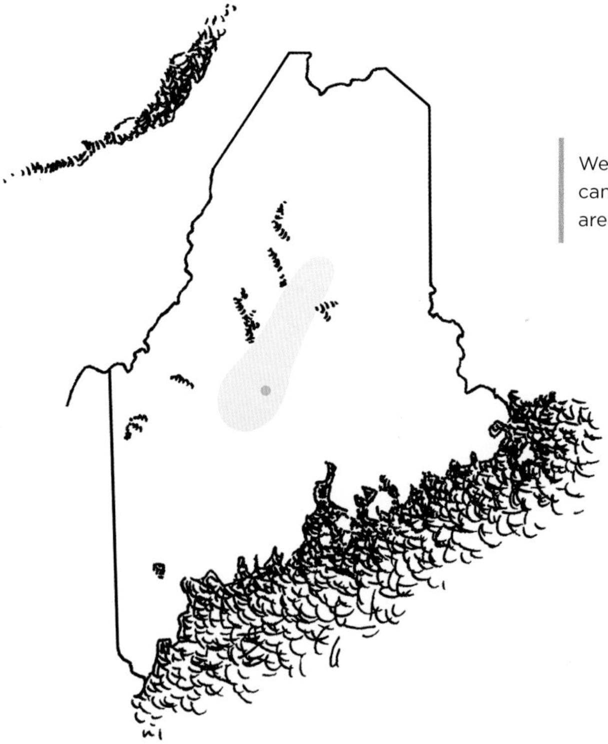

Wedge-ledge chompers can be found in rocky areas of central Maine.

Not too much else is known about these shy and peaceful creatures, which seem to only be found in the hills and mountains of central Maine. At least a small population of these secretive creatures still lives on the mountains around the west end of Sebec Lake. They may be a distant cousin to the much larger and more dangerous slide-rock bolter of the western United States. Those large, fearsome creatures hang from steep cliff sides and slide down to devour unsuspecting people and causing rockslides.

*"It's settled for me now—those boulders are not in the same spot they were yesterday. I suspect they aren't actually boulders at all."*

—Burton Marlborough Packard, 1920

# WEEWILLMEKQ

## Wabanaki Creature

This mysterious and powerful water creature was perhaps the most feared and honored creature of the ancient Wabanaki. Only a fool would seek it out of curiosity alone.

**GREAT HORNED** water serpents are common in accounts of Native Americans across the continent. In traditional Wabanaki stories, the *weewillmekq* (or *chepechcalm* in Micmac) is one of the most powerful and dangerous creatures of the region. Its large head has fiery eyes that shine with an inhuman intelligence and its mouth is filled with sharp teeth. Its slimy body is more slug than snake, and its horns are forked like a deer's antlers but are soft and retractable.

While not evil, the *weewillmekq* is still terribly dangerous. Those who meet it must face not only its powerful body and poisonous slime but also its cunning and magic.

These creatures are said to be the rulers of the world below the surface. In its natural form, this water worm is large, but, like many Wabanaki creatures, it has the ability to change its shape or size. On land, it can become small enough to be easily mistaken for an ordinary slug. The *weewillmekq* can also change into human form to help it seduce human prey, and some say this human shape is what it wears when it lives deep below. Despite its size and power, it spends much of its time hiding secretly underwater away from thunder giants, who are its mortal enemies. *Weewillmekq* can be found in the ocean, large lakes, deep pools below waterfalls, and even the water below a spring. When they come to land, they leave deep, muddy trenches; it is said that these trenches are the gateways to the *weewillmekq*'s world.

The *weewillmekq*'s source of power and magic is its horns. One horn is said to be red and the other yellow. If taken, these can be powerful weapons and are capable of slaying any foe or monster. Scrapings of the horns can be used to cure or cause any curse or illness, even the dreaded wendigo curse. However, a *weewillmekq* won't give up its magic to the weak or fearful. As a last resort, desperate people sometimes summon the *weewillmekq* to ask for its aid. The *weewillmekq* can communicate with those who summon it and will grant a favor to those whom they deem worthy. But only the bravest and truest of heart can meet the *weewillmekq*'s gaze without becoming its prey. The words to an ancient Wabanaki song to summon this creature were recorded by Charles Leland in the late 1800s. Other stories also talk of summoning them by singing and drumming on the water with a stick.

| | |
|---|---|
| *We que moh wee will l'mick,* | I call on the Wee-will-l'mick! |
| *We que moh m'cha micso,* | I call on the Terrible One! |
| *Som'awo wee will l'mick!* | On the One with the Horns! |
| *Cardup ke su m'so wo Sawo!* | I dare him to appear! |

Because of its power, Wabanaki shamans and sorcerers have sometimes taken the form of this creature or summoned it as their spirit helper. One famous story tells of Penobscot governor John Neptune taking the form of a *weewillmekq* to battle an evil sorcerer from another tribe. His opponent took the form of a giant lake serpent. The encounter took place at Boyden Lake in Waldo County and ended with the lake forever muddied. Neptune emerged from the battle victorious but exhausted and covered with the fishy slime of the *weewillmekq*.

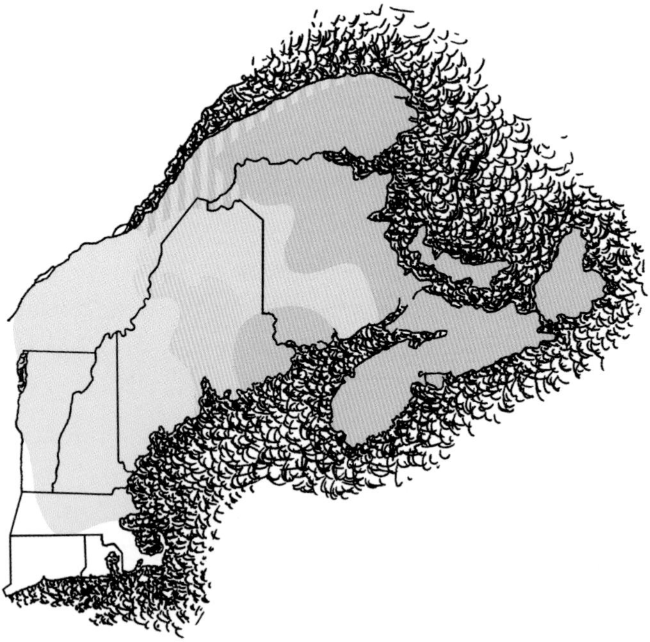

*Weewillmekq* can be found in waters throughout traditional Wabanaki territory: Micmac (purple), Maliseet (blue), Passamaquoddy (brown), Penobscot (pink), Abenaki (green).

# WENDIGO

## Wabanaki Creature and Fearsome Critter of the Lumberwoods

These wild and evil cannibal giants sometimes roam the area in winter. They are as greedy and hungry as they are powerful. Wendigos are creatures of fear.

**THE WENDIGO** is a creature of ice and terror. These cannibal giants are wild and solitary forest dwellers with a monstrous appetite for destruction and human flesh. They wander lonely forests across Canada and come down into the northern United States during winter. It is said that they follow the blowing of the cold north wind. Wendigos look half-starved and are covered in dirty hair, matted with hardened sap and leaves. Driven by an insatiable hunger for human flesh, they are powerful and cunning.

Early lumbermen greatly feared the wendigo and its taste for human flesh. Loggers avoided the forest pools where wendigos were said to live and would search the snow for the wendigo's long footprints. Their prints were said to always have a spot of blood in the center. Even a rumor of the wendigo could stop work for a season—for this reason, sometimes competing lumbermen would make fake wendigo tracks using fur-covered snowshoes and a drop of cow blood.

While known to lumbermen of the Northeast, *wendigo* is actually a Native American word of the Algonquin people to the west. The New England Wabanaki call these creatures variously *chenoo*, *djenu*, or *kiwakw*. In their normal form, they are small giants at eight to ten feet in height, though, like many Wabanaki creatures, they have magical powers and the ability to change their size. Wendigos have been recorded changing their size from that of a normal human to a giant large enough to uproot full-size trees and swing them as weapons. It turns out the only thing the cannibal wendigo loves to hunt more than humans is other wendigos. If two of them meet, they will grow to enormous size and fight to the death, creating great destruction all around. During their battles, their shrill howls can be heard for miles. Ideally you will never hear one, because their screams shake the very land and can be fatal to those who hear them.

A *chenoo* is shown hunting a giant lizard he has summoned up from a spring in an 1884 birch-bark etching by Wabanaki artist Tomah Josephs.

Wendigos are almost never caught by surprise, as they have a keen sense of smell and their little finger is said to be gifted with the magical ability to warn them of danger.

Female wendigos are more powerful than males. But no matter the gender, their power comes from their magical heart of ice. This ice is as much colder than normal ice "as ice is colder than fire" and as much harder than normal ice "as ice is harder than water." If a wendigo is killed, its heart must be melted and its body burned, for even the smallest piece can regenerate into a new wendigo.

Much like the *loup garou*, wendigos are not a race of creatures, but rather humans who have been cursed. In many ways, the heart of the curse is selfishness and greed. It is said that their hunger is such that the more they eat, the hungrier they feel. They can never be satisfied, so they can never rest. Sometimes a foolish and power-hungry sorcerer will cast the wendigo spell on himself to gain a terrible power. But most wendigos did not choose this fate. The most common cause for the curse is cannibalism, but some are afflicted when an angry sorcerer casts the curse upon a victim. The first signs that a person has the wendigo curse is that they become bad tempered, spend much time alone, and complain about warm temperatures. Eventually they will lose their appetite for normal food. There is little hope for one struck by the wendigo curse.

Modern psychology sometimes recognizes a disorder known as the Wendigo Psychosis, which strikes most frequently in winter. The condition is typically characterized as a two-stage disorder: At first, the affected person becomes depressed and withdrawn and loses their appetite. Next, they become violent, murderous, and obsessed with eating human flesh. This cannibalistic psychosis is said to be unique to the northern Algonquin cultural group, typically those north and northwest of the Wabanaki lands. One of the earliest descriptions of the disorder was provided by French Jesuit missionaries in central Quebec. The account from 1661 is translated below:

They are afflicted with neither lunacy, hypochondria, nor frenzy; but have a combination of all these species of disease, which affects their imaginations and causes them a more than canine hunger. This makes them so ravenous for human flesh that they pounce upon women, children, and even upon men, like veritable werewolves, and devour them voraciously, without being able to appease or glut their appetite—ever seeking fresh prey, and the more greedily the more they eat. This ailment attacked our deputies; and, as death is the sole remedy among those simple people for checking such acts of murder, the deputies were slain in order to stay the course of their madness.

—Unknown French Jesuit Missionary, 1661

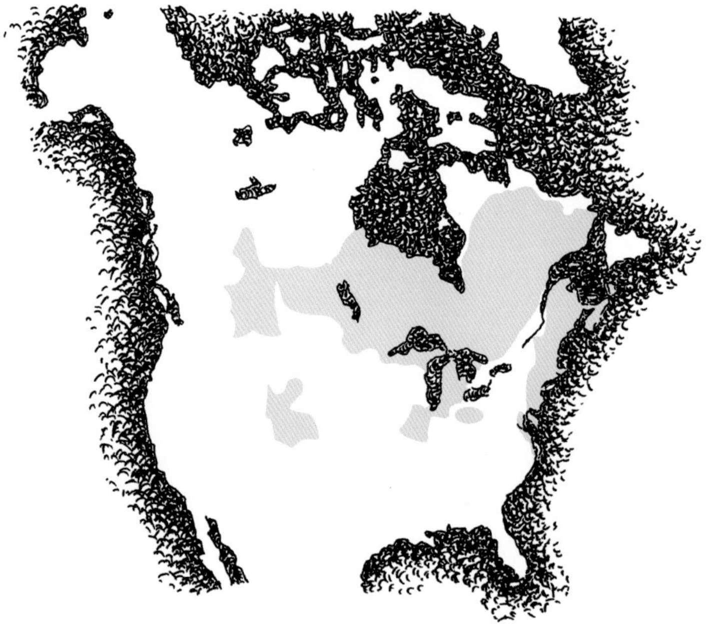

The wendigo is known throughout the traditional territory of the Algonquin Native American cultural group (blue), but it is especially common in the northern areas.

The association of the wendigo with mental illness is undoubtedly an attempt by colonists and scientists alike to understand what is clearly a real occurrence in the area. The comparison to the werewolf, or *loup garou*, perhaps tells of a universal theme or affliction. Whether curse, witchcraft, or possession by the wendigo spirit, this creature of the icy northern forests is very real.

> *"They were going to start logging up near Big Benson Pond this winter, but a set of giant footprints in the snow has shut the operation down. There are whispers of a wendigo."*
>
> —Burton Marlborough Packard, 1899

# WILL-AM-ALONE

## Fearsome Critter of the Lumberwoods

(*Incomitatus venenarius*)

**NOT MUCH** is known about this strange little creature except for its troublesome habit of dropping poisonous lichen balls into the ears and eyelids of sleeping people. The poisonous

Be careful where you fall asleep, or the troublesome will-am-alone will take revenge on you for trespassing in his forest.

balls cause the victim to have strange dreams and headaches and to see visions in the snow. The best cure for this poison is the fat of the side-hill gouger.

The will-am-alone is very secretive and usually only glimpsed out of the corner of the eye. While it seems very similar in size and appearance to a squirrel, it is a clever and purposeful creature. It is best known from descriptions from early lumber camps, where lumberjacks who drank too much liquor were the ones most often attacked by the will-am-alones. These creatures are only known from the deep woods of Maine, and they were once much more common than they are today.

Some similarity with the will-am-alone might be drawn to a species of little people known as the *mikumwesuk*. These forest spirits are also small, secretive, and sometimes described as hairy. While usually harmless,

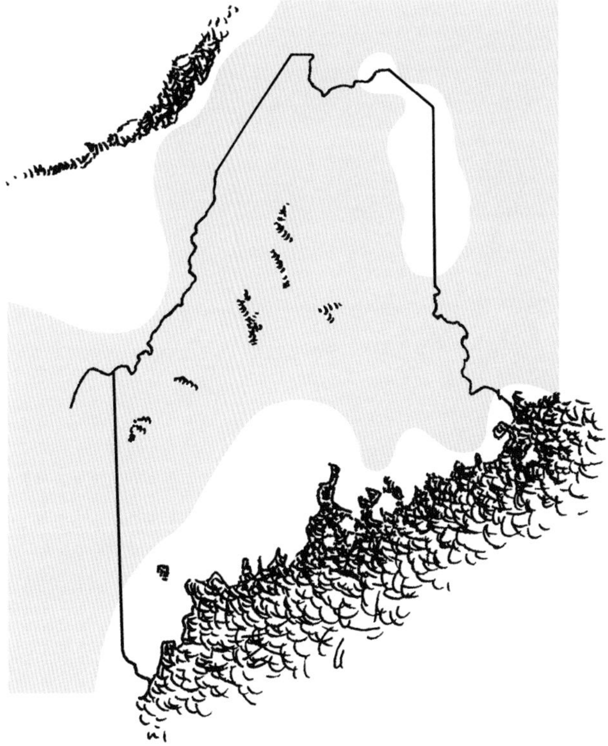

Will-am-alones can be found throughout Maine's lumberwoods.

they can be quite protective of their territories, especially if disrespected. It's certainly easy to understand why these forest spirits might not take kindly to the activities of lumbermen. In one old Wabanaki tale, it was said that guardian *mikumwesuk* would "push the brains out" of unsuspecting trespassers they found. Fear of these attacks prompted Wabanaki hunters sleeping outside in unfamiliar territory to protect themselves by using their snowshoes to make a lean-to over their heads. Compared to a wary native hunter, drunken lumbermen would certainly be easy targets.

> *"All I have to say is be careful where you sleep."*
> —Burton Marlborough Packard, 1931

# WILL O' THE WISP

## Old World and Wabanaki Creature

(*Ignis fatuus*)

**WILL O' THE WISPS** appear as ghostly dancing lights that can be seen moving through forests and bogs around the world. They are almost always seen at night near water and wet ground. Always staying just ahead of those

A will o' the wisp looks like a ball of light floating through the forest, leading a person into a swamp.

who pursue them, no one knows the origin of these lights. Some believe that they are lanterns carried by ghosts or fairies. Others think they are glowing otherworldly spirits or the spirit helpers of witches or shamans.

Whatever their cause, their purpose is equally mysterious. Some say that their aim is to lead travelers astray, never to be seen again. Others say they are harmless fairy pranks or tormented ghosts who are unaware of the living. Will o' the wisps are also sometimes seen as forerunners (or portents) of death and bad luck. In English, other names for them are "marsh fires" or "jack o' lanterns." The French Acadians call them *feux follet*, or fairy fires, and they often chase people rather than lead them astray. Quebecois French Canadians sometimes call them *feu volant*, which means "flying fire." These creatures spook horses and humans alike. The *feu volant* specifically are said to be a bird-like creatures that fly backward to avoid getting branches and dust in their eyes. This idea of a backward-flying bird corresponds

The mischievous fairy Puck is shown acting as a will o' the wisp and leading people astray in Arthur Rackham's 1908 illustration for Shakespeare's *A Midsummer Night's Dream*.

to a lumber creature called the Philly Lou Bird (or Filla-ma-lou Bird), which flies backward because it doesn't care where it's going—it only wants to look back at where it's been. This clumsy bird is also said to build its nest upside down. It's not difficult to see how the French word *feux follet* (pronounced "few few-lae") could change into Philly Lou when spoken by English-speaking lumberjacks. While the names are clearly related, it's unclear how a backward bird creature and a nocturnal fairy light are related. These French and English names were certainly carried here with settlers from Europe, but the phenomenon of flying lights is well known to the native Wabanaki as well.

In Henry David Thoreau's classic work, *The Maine Woods*, Thoreau's guide, a Penobscot, responds to his inquiries about will o' the wisps by saying that his "folks sometimes saw fires passing along at various heights, even as high as the trees, and making a noise." Like their European counterparts, the Wabanaki generally saw them as an omen of bad luck or

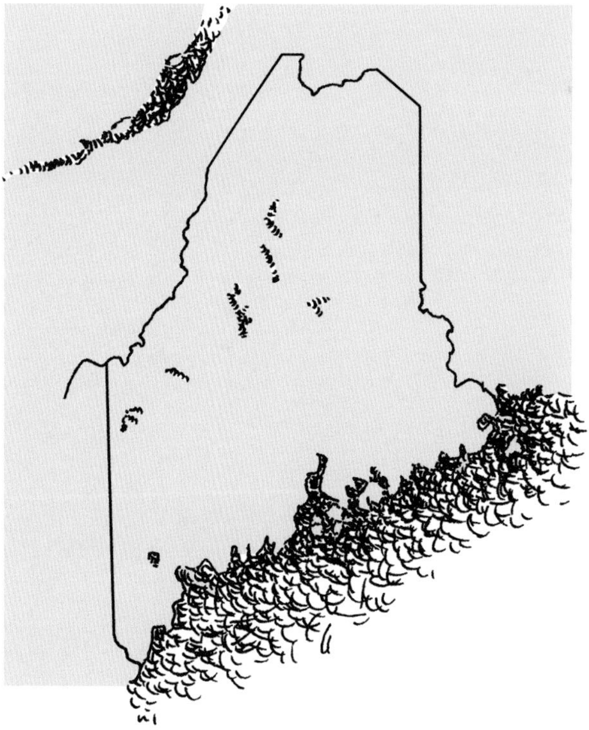

Will o' the wisps can be found throughout North America, Europe, and beyond.

death. Historical Wabanaki stories describe will o' the wisps as ghosts or the out-of-body spirit of a sorcerer that, instead of leading people astray, pursues and attacks people. Wabanaki terms used for these types of creatures are *gas'top* or *skadegamutc*. The latter is sometimes translated as a "ghost witch" and is said to be the spirit of an evil sorcerer who refuses to stay dead and haunts the land at night. Another Wabanaki creature similar to the will o' the wisp is the Penobscot *eskuda'hit*. These "fire creatures" are summoned by shamans as spirit helpers. They appear as flying lights, and through the flames some have seen them as having snake-like bodies with large faces and scars on their cheeks.

> *"These otherworldly lights of the night can pursue or lead astray, but my best advice is to simply stay away."*
>
> —Burton Marlborough Packard, 1893

## Appendix A

# THE CULTURAL MYTHOLOGY OF MAINE

**THE CREATURES** in this book represent the creatures and people that make up the mythology of the region. Mythology in this case is not meant in the sense of "a widely held but false belief or idea." Instead, it is meant as a traditional story that embodies a belief regarding some fact or phenomenon of experience. Myths are cultural information; they are the living soul of a society and place. The stories that make up myths help us share cultural truths and lessons; they create a sense of place and meaning within the world. Myths can be conveyed through religion, media, or the oral tradition of storytelling. Because of its history of colonization and immigration, America has a strange and somewhat disjointed and ephemeral mythology created by layering culture upon culture within a place followed by the introduction of mass information media before a solid mythological identity could fully take hold. In order to survive, the creatures and peoples populating America's myths have had to change and adapt as the times changed.

Originally, there was only Wabanaki mythology here, closely tied to the land and the language of the area's First People. The beings that populate these myths are mostly nature spirits with magical powers. They include several races of elves and dwarves, serpents, birds, spirits, floating lights, and giant people and creatures of various sorts.

### WABANAKI

- Giants
- Lake Serpent
- Little People, Forest Elves (*Mikumwesuk*)
- Little People, River Elves (*Manogamasak*)
- Little People, Silent Elves (*Kiwolatomuhsisok*)
- Little People, Stone Dwarves (*Wiklatmu'j*)
- Mermaid (*Lumpeguin*)
- Mermaid (*Nodumkanwet*)
- Pamola
- *Weewillmekq*
- Wendigo
- Will o' the Wisp

Next came European settlers. First on the scene were the French Acadians of Nova Scotia, New Brunswick, and Down East Maine. They brought their mythology with them, and some of their creatures were on the ships with these settlers. But these Acadians were soon displaced into the wilds by the English. They and their mythology mixed quite thoroughly with the Wabanaki, who were also being displaced. Today, the Canadian government even recognizes these people as an Indigenous First People called the *Mètis*. The Wabanaki, French Acadians, and Mètis were joined by the later-arriving Quebecois French; their language was a little different, but their mythology was much the same. Meanwhile, in Nova Scotia, New Brunswick, and Maine (south of the Kennebec River), the English and other British peoples were arriving, and they brought their mythology, much of it not so different from that of the French.

### FRENCH

- Little People (Lutin)
- *Loup Garou*

- Mermaid
- Sea Serpent
- Will o' the Wisp

### ENGLISH

- Bigfoot (Wildmen)
- Little People
- Mermaid
- Sea Serpent
- Will o' the Wisp

Eventually the British fully gained control of the area and largely forgot their mythology, while the French remembered theirs. By the 1800s, all the groups had mixed and moved around. They associated as woodsmen and lumbermen. Some of the mythology remained and evolved. But much new mythology was discovered by these lumbermen—these are the "Fearsome Critters of the Lumberwoods." Their mythology reflects quite clearly a close but adversarial, dangerous, and unfamiliar relationship with the land. It was meant to bring them together, celebrate their values, and warn them of dangers. Today we call these "tall tales" instead of myths. Many people think no one could ever have believed them, but people did believe, and they carried these creatures with them as mythology west across the continent.

### FEARSOME CRITTERS OF THE LUMBERWOODS

- Agropelter
- Billdad
- Celofay
- Come-at-a-body
- Ding-ball
- Dingmaul
- Dungavenhooter
- Gazerium and Snydae

- Hide-behind
- Kaput Bird
- Landlocked Walrus
- Little People
- *Lunksoos*
- Pamola
- Sidehill Gouger
- Snipe
- Snow Snake
- Specter Moose
- Tote Road Shagamaw
- Tree Squeak
- Wamfahoofus
- Wedge-ledge Chomper
- Wendigo
- Will-am-alone

Then we come to today. Many of us are only visitors on the land now; we live a life inspired instead by television, the internet, and memes. Though some of us still remember our past mythologies, it would do us good if we all could. It seems that's the way we're headed—some of our mythology has returned through the very media that distracted us from it in the first place. But a new mythology has emerged as well: cryptozoology—a field of science dedicated to looking for creatures believed to be real animals but as yet unknown to science. Interestingly, many of the cryptid creatures are echoes of our past mythologies. Perhaps they are waking up, calling for people to come looking for them. Some might say they're different from the "tall tale" fearsome critters of the lumberwoods, but they're no different than the world itself is from the world of that time. Aside from cryptozoology, there are other traditional supernatural creatures that many modern people know quite well. Some are in this book, but, in addition to those that fall within the scope of this project, there are mythological beings such as angels, ghosts, aliens, and demons.

### CRYPTID CREATURES

- Bigfoot
- Lake Serpent
- Mountain Lion
- Sea Serpent
- Turner Beast

### MODERN MYTHOLOGICAL CREATURES

- Fairies
- Ice Hornet
- Sidehill Gouger
- Snipe
- Snow Snake
- Tree Squeak
- Wamfahoofus
- Wendigo

Many people wonder whether these mythical creatures and beings exist, even if we don't believe in them. I think they exist, no matter what, but we just don't recognize them anymore. It's easy to miss what you aren't looking for or to mistake it for something else. People who are not used to being in the woods can easily overlook an animal or flower that might seem in plain view to someone familiar with the outdoors. I've seen people walk right under a porcupine in a tree, nearly step on a frog or a snake, even miss a moose standing just off the path. These were all people who were not used to looking for the wonders around them. Once they learned to see animals, tracks, or certain plants, they began to find them. That's how these creatures are—if you don't know to look for them, you won't see them.

Appendix B

# BURTON MARLBOROUGH PACKARD (1864–1945)

**MY GREAT-GREAT**-grandfather Burton Marlborough Packard's "quotes" are featured in this book. To me he is the embodiment of the Maine woodsman and entrepreneur at the turn of the twentieth century. He was exactly the type of person who would have encountered the creatures in this book. In 1864, he was born in Searsport to a well-known and influential shipbuilder. He grew up familiar with the sea and knew many sailors, sea captains, and fishermen who would have introduced him to mermaids and sea serpents. His own adventures in the shipping business didn't end so well; his investments in ships were all uninsured and ended up at the bottom of the sea.

Hearing that the lumber business was booming, he ventured in that direction. He spent a couple winters cutting and peeling pulpwood. However, he didn't meet much success in this regard, being swindled out of the profit by his partner the first year and losing a winter's cutting in a forest fire the next. As a lumberman, he would have met firsthand some of these fearsome lumberwood creatures during his time in the logging camp. In particular, the puckish Sock Saunders seems to have paid him a visit.

After that, he bought a pistol and a horse and headed west to Minnesota, where he drove a stagecoach and lost his savings in an ill-advised poker gamble. I can't imagine what types of creatures he'd have met there, but Minnesota is also a hotbed of lumber creatures.

He then headed back to Maine and got a job as a fireman and night watchman in the Willimantic Spool Mill in the booming town of Willimantic. Eventually he came to run the company boarding house and store. By 1894, he had saved enough money to purchase an interesting property down the way called the Lake House. It would later become Packard's Camps at Packard's Landing. When he bought it, there was a rustic hotel, a farm, a two-lane bowling alley, and a small plot of land leased as a four-home "French Settlement" near the spool mill. These French tenants would have known all about lutins and *loup garou*.

Aside from the millworkers, his hotel and camps served lumbermen, trappers, hunters, blueberry pickers, timber cruisers, spruce-gum pickers, river drivers, fishermen, sportsmen, city rusticators, and travelers of all other sorts. If it existed in the Maine woods, these were the people who knew about it. And right in the hotel he employed three full-time Maine guides: Sam McKenny, Harvey Hurd, and Ruben Riley. Guides are full of stories of unlikely adventures. Burton Marlborough himself was no stranger to woodscraft—each fall he and Sam McKenny would spend six weeks in a log cabin four miles north of the hotel, hunting and trapping for extra income.

Later, especially after the mill closed in 1903, the Lake House became a full-fledged wilderness hotel with over a dozen freestanding camps that would cater to wealthy urbanites eager to get away into nature, country stories, and sporting adventures. There were many of these wilderness resort hotels across Maine at the time. Packard's Lake Hotel and Cottages was a small but worthy member of this cohort. I'm certain he met all sorts during this time. My grandfather even told me that when he was a boy, "Indians" would come by each year to gather sweetgrass along the river behind the hotel, which they likely used for making baskets.

The hotel and cottages continued to operate as a family business called Packard's Camps for over one hundred years. Unlike many of the

Burton Marlborough Packard on the road behind Packard's Camps, circa 1920.

other wilderness hotels, it still stands. However, today only memories visit the hotel as it looks over the head of Sebec Lake. Many of Burton Marlborough's descendants still frequent the lake, and several still live in Willimantic.

Of course, because his life was so full of experiences, he never did get a chance to write anything down about these creatures. In fact, he never wrote much of anything other than publicity material for his hotel. Nonetheless, knowledge of these creatures was carried to me through a well-tended family tradition of woodscraft and storytelling. These traditions are some of the best parts of what makes Maine special. Some things in Maine have changed over the years, but thankfully that has not.

## Appendix C

# WABANAKI LANGUAGES AND CULTURE

**MANY OF** the creatures in this book are Wabanaki and thus have Wabanaki names, so it's important to understand a little about the Wabanaki languages in order to fully understand these creatures. First of all, Wabanaki languages are closely related, as they are all part of the Algonquin language group. There are at least three Wabanaki languages: Penobscot-Abenaki, Passamaquoddy-Maliseet, and Micmac; each has or had multiple dialects. Of the three, Micmac is the most different. Prior to European contact, these languages were only spoken and not written down, and they are fundamentally different from European languages. This difference made early translation into English quite unreliable and often confused or contradictory. Most of the records from which my research was done transcribed the Wabanaki phonetically and often with different phonetic systems. This, along with the multiple languages and dialects, often made piecing together the stories of these creatures difficult. It would not have been possible without the wonderful website of the Minnesota-based nonprofit Native Languages of the Americas (native-languages.org).

Conceptually, language fundamentally and subconsciously shapes our worldview. Because of this, those of us who only speak English or most other European languages all share somewhat similar ways of thinking about the world. Most of us are probably not even aware of how language shapes thinking. European languages tend to be noun oriented; verbs are mostly there just to move nouns around. However, Wabanaki and other Algonquin languages are often called verb-oriented languages, though they do have nouns. The nouns that are used have an interesting animate-inanimate conjugation (similar to gender conjugation in French or Spanish). However, unlike the gender conjugation, which generally only has a grammatical function, Wabanaki animate-inanimate conveys information about the object. For instance, a pair of snowshoes might be expressed not as a fixed non-living object but as an animate or enspirited being that would translate to "one being snowshoes," making these nouns quite verb-like.

Additionally, true verbs in Wabanaki conjugate into present, distant past, uncertain, absent, and other tenses that add rich shades of meaning to the concept being expressed. The verbs can also be combined with prefixes and suffixes and can even be combined with other words. In some cases, the words become very long, and often an entire sentence can be expressed with a single well-conjugated verb. In this way, it is somewhat similar to the German language, which allows words to be compounded into new words freely. These compound words give a more specific or nuanced meaning. In German, however, the new word is always a noun, referring to a fixed object or concept, even if it has a long and descriptive name.

This Wabanaki language, with few "fixed" words and animate-inanimate nouns, changes the very nature of the universe from one full of things to one full of beings and becomings. It reflects a concept that the world is constantly creating itself rather than just existing. This concept is fundamental to my understanding of the magical powers of the Wabanaki creatures. Because of this, no animal, plant, or creature is simply a "thing" in Wabanaki; they are all people with a power to choose and create. Nearly all the Wabanaki creatures in this book have the power to transform into new shapes, change their size, bring themselves back from the dead, walk into stone, explore the sky, live underwater, or converse with humans. In a world understood by Wabanaki language, which is a formative language rather than a fixed one, this is all normal and makes sense. The language is not fixed; therefore, the world, so clearly full of natural transformations and cycles, is not fixed either.

Throughout this book, three prefixes and suffixes are used frequently in creature names. Because of the differences in Wabanaki languages and the somewhat nonstandardized way to render them, you will see them spelled differently throughout, but the meaning always remains the same. The table below is a very simplified and generalized way to recognize these important prefixes and suffixes.

| PREFIX/SUFFIX | MEANING |
|---|---|
| Kci- Kchi- Tci- Kji- | A prefix often translated as "great." It denotes power and size (which are related). |
| -sis -wes -as -es, -ess, -si's | A diminutive suffix meaning "small." Sometimes applied to distinguish between a mythic character and a creature or being currently found in the world. |
| -ak, -uk, -ok, -u'k | A suffix used to make a word plural or indicate the entirety of a people or species. |

As an example, there's a Wabanaki mythic creature that is a giant bird that preys on humans and lives in the sky. In Micmac, this creature is called the *Kulu*. In fact, *Kulu* is a chief of a whole village of these bird creatures; these people are the *Kulu'k*. And the chief is the oldest, largest, and most powerful; he is *Kji'kulu*. The youngest son of the chief is very young and very small; he is called *Kulusi's*.

One final note on language: Since language was not the focus of this project, I have relied heavily on other works. *Stories from the Six Worlds* by Ruth Holmes Whitehead was instrumental in my conceptual understanding of the Wabanaki languages and worldview at the outset of this project. This book was the first I encountered that really helped me understand how very little I knew about Algonquin language and culture. And the Wabanaki elements of this work would have been far more difficult and confusing without the comprehensive website native-languages.org. This source was typically my final authority for both spelling and pronunciation of Wabanaki words. In that regard, when a word was shared between two languages (typically Penobscot and Passamoquoddy), I have only given one pronunciation; typically I chose Passamaquoddy. In most cases, I have labeled them simply as "a" Wabanaki pronunciation. I encourage you to refer to the original website (or a native speaker) if you need to know for certain which I used.

It is impossible to understand the Wabanaki magical beings without understanding their culture, which cannot be done properly unless it is directly from them. Therefore, I cannot recommend enough that if you have an interest in this area, you investigate it through resources from the Wabanaki nations and people directly. By themselves, the translations and transcriptions of their stories by folklorists, anthropologists, and the ministry are not a reliable way to come to fully understand them. The cultural and linguistic differences between Europeans and the Wabanaki were (and are) simply too great for these deep, multifaceted stories and teachings to be conveyed fully and accurately. I am not a Wabanaki, and despite my best efforts and intentions, I am certain I have made some of the same mistakes as the folklorists who came before me. For mistakes I have made in this regard, I apologize. I don't claim to be an expert; I merely wish to celebrate and honor the Wabanaki culture that is so deeply woven into this place we all love. It should also be known that some elements I learned about Wabanaki beliefs have been left out of this book. In particular, I have omitted any information from Wabanaki ceremonies I have attended as well as that gained through informal conversations with a Wabanaki person. I am grateful for these gifts, and I recognize in turn that those living traditions are not mine to share. I encourage you to seek out these very real people on your own, as I will continue to do.

## Books by Wabanaki and Algonquin Cultural Group Authors

*Modern Fiction by an Abenaki Author Using Traditional Themes and Storytelling*

Bruchac, J. 1993. *Dawnland: A Novel.* Golden, CO: Fulcrum Publishing.

Bruchac, J. 2009. *Night Wings.* New York: HarperCollins.

Bruchac, J., & J. Bruchac. 1998. *When the Chenoo Howls: Native American Tales of Terror.* New York: Walker and Company.

*Traditional Tales*

Mead, A., & A. Neptune. 1996. *Giants of the Dawnland: Ancient Wabanaki Tales*. Cumberland Center, ME: Loose Cannon Press.

*Nonfictional Works about Wabanaki Culture, Language, and Philosophy*

Mitchell, S. 2018. *Sacred Instructions: Indigenous Wisdom for Living Spirit-Based Change*. Berkeley, CA: North Atlantic Books.

Nicolar, J. 1893. *The Life and Traditions of the Red Man*. Bangor, ME: C.H. Glass & Co. Printers. Available at archive.org/details/lifeandtraditio00nicogoog/page/n8.

Sable, T., & B. Francis. 2012. *The Language of This Land Mi'kma'ki*. Halifax: Cape Breton University Press.

*Nonfiction Works about Related Algonquin Cultural Groups*

Johnston, B. 1995. *Manitous: The Spiritual World of the Ojibway*. New York: HarperCollins.

Kimmer, R. W. 2013. *Braiding Sweetgrass: Indigenous Wisdom, Scientific Knowledge, and the Teachings of Plants*. Minneapolis, MN: Milkweed Editions.

## Maine Wabanaki Museums, Events, and Cultural Centers

*Abbe Museum: A Smithsonian Affiliate*

The Abbe Museum reflects and realizes the values of decolonization in all of its practices, working with the Wabanaki Nations to share their stories, history, and culture with a broader audience. Many permanent exhibits, events, and a satellite location in Acadia National Park.

26 Mt Desert Street, P.O. Box 286, Bar Harbor, ME 04609; 207-288-3519; info@abbemuseum.org; abbemuseum.org/

*Aroostook Band of Micmacs*

The band hosts an annual Mawiomi (gathering) of tribes on the third weekend in August. The Aroostook Band of Micmacs celebrates all people of Mother Earth. It also operates a museum located within the Micmac Cultural Community Education Center.

7 Northern Road, Presque Isle, ME 04769; 207-764-1972; micmac-nsn.gov/index.html

*Nibezun: Wabanaki Cultural Center*

Nibezun resides on sacred Wabanaki land along the Penobscot River, where it celebrates culture as medicine, provides an inclusive space for healing, and promotes sustainability for all people and future generations. The center hosts regular educational events.

18 Nepisikwit Drive, Passadumkeag, ME 04475; 207-659-3926; nibezun.org

*Penobscot Nation Museum*

The Penobscot Nation Museum is dedicated to preserving and sharing the rich cultural heritage of the Penobscot and Wabanaki peoples.

12 Down Street, Old Town, ME; 207-827-4153; museum@penobscotnation.org; penobscotnation.org/penobscot-nation-museum

*Waponahki Museum and Resource Center*

The center's mission is to preserve the Passamaquoddy tribal culture and traditions for future generations.

59 Passamaquoddy Road, Pleasant Point, ME 04667; 207-853-2600, ext. 227; wabanaki.com/wabanaki_new/Museum.html

# COMPREHENSIVE GLOSSARY OF MYTHICAL MAINE CREATURES

*Aglebemu* (ah-gluh-beh-moo): A giant frog or reptilian creature of Wabanaki myth that made the rivers go dry by swallowing all the water; he was defeated by Gluskap. Sometimes referred to as *Kci-cekolhs*, which literally means "giant frog."

Agropelter: This fearsome critter of the lumberwoods is a small tree-dwelling ape that throws branches at passersby with deadly accuracy.

*Alambaguenosis* (ah-lam-peh-gwinn; plural: *alambaguenosisak*): Penobscot name for a small mermaid. See *Lumpeguin*; Mermaids.

*Apodumken* (ah-boo-dahm-kun): A fanged sea serpent or large mermaid of Passamaquoddy Bay and the St. Croix River. Perhaps the same as the Penobscot *nodumkanwet*. See Mermaids.

*Asinikiwakw* (ah-seh-neh-keh-wah-kwah): An ancient race of stone-skinned man-eating giants found in Abenaki myths. Their name seems to be derived from the *kiwakw* (wendigo).

*Atwuskniges* (ah-too-wuss-kuh-nee-gass): A powerful Wabanaki giant or forest spirit from the mythological age who fells trees with his stone axe and is friends with a great turtle who aids him in the water. See Giants.

*Badogiak* (puh-dawn-gee-uck, singular: *badogi*): A race of Wabanaki thunder giants. See Giants.

Ball-tailed Cat: An alternative name for the ding-ball in Pennsylvania and Oregon. See Ding-ball; Dingmaul.

Bigfoot: Perhaps the best-known mysterious creature of modern times, bigfoot is a missing-link creature between humans and apes.

Billdad: Found only in Boundary Pond, this is Maine's answer to the platypus. Part beaver, part kangaroo, and part hawk, this shy little creature makes its living hunting fish with its tail.

*B'mole*: The first recorded spelling of Pamola. See Pamola.

*Bochdan*: A British hobgoblin brought to the area by Scottish immigrants; also spelled *bauchan*. They're quite similar to lutins. See Little People; Lutin.

Cassie: A nickname for a sea serpent known from the Casco Bay area.

Catamount: An alternative name for the mountain lion. See Mountain Lion.

Celofay: A fearsome ventriloquist cat that throws its screams in order to panic its prey.

Champ: A nickname for the very well-known lake serpent found in Lake Champlain.

*Chebelaque* (chee-buh-lock-w; alternate spellings: *tci'pilakw* or *geebellowk*): A dangerous spirit of the night air of the Wabanaki. It appears as a large-eyed bird creature. See Pamola.

*Chenoo* (cheh-noo): A Wabanaki name for the wendigo. See Wendigo.

*Chepechcalm* (chih-pitch-kawm): An alternate spelling of *jipijka'm* or *kchi pitchkayam*, a horned sea or lake serpent or dragon of the Micmac. See Lake Serpents; Sea Serpent; *Weewillmekq*.

Cherryfield Goatman: A satyr-like cryptid first appearing in a story published in a book of folklore called *New England Graveside Tales* by T. M. Gray (2010) and later propagated across the internet. Upon investigation, I was unable to find any corroborating reports from the Cherryfield, Maine, area.

Come-at-a-body: A cute and fuzzy but foul-tempered critter that startles woodsmen by rushing at them from the bushes—found only in the White Mountains.

Cougar: The official name of the mountain lion (*Puma concolor*), a large wildcat that was once found across North America. Despite persistent sightings, it is officially listed as extinct in the Northeast.

*Culloo* (kuh-loo): A giant bird of Wabanaki myth sometimes said to be capable of flying off with people or even small moose. Some anthropologists think this is a reference to golden eagles (*Aquila chrysaetos*).

Ding-ball: A medium-sized wildcat with a deadly bony ball on the end of its tail.

Dingmaul: This fearsome but harmless creature is a very large cat with a bony ball on its long tail, which it uses to break trees and for mating purposes.

*Djenu*: An alternate Micmac spelling of *chenoo*, a Wabanaki name for the wendigo. See Wendigo.

Dungavenhooter: A large reptilian creature with no mouth, this fearsome critter eats by pulverizing its victims and snorting them up through its nose. The similarly named dungarvin whooper is a well-known whooping ghost in New Brunswick and Maine.

*Eskuda'hit* (es-kwe-duh-hit): A Wabanaki fire creature, which is summoned by shamans as a spirit helper. Associated with will o' the wisps.

Fairies: Tiny whimsical nature spirits who likely immigrated from Europe, they love the tiny homes people build for them.

*Feu Volant* (few vu-laen): A haunting spirit of the Quebec Canadians that spooked lumberjack horses at night. This spirit light's name literally means "flying fire," though it is often described as a bird-like creature that flies backward through the woods to avoid getting branches and dust in its eyes. See Will o' the Wisp.

*Feux Follet* (few few-lae): A French word for the will o' the wisp, literally translating to "fairy fire."

Forest Elves: A small but powerful race of Wabanaki forest spirits that are always watching but rarely seen. Their Wabanaki name is *mikumwesuk*. See Little People.

Gazerium: This three-legged shrimp of the Kennebec tastes like cocktail sauce and is part of a circular food chain with the snydae.

*Geebellowk* (chee-buh-lock-w; alternate spellings: *tci'pilakw* or *chebelaque*): A dangerous Wabanaki spirit of the night air. It appears as a large-eyed, bird-like creature. See Pamola.

Giants: Any of several types of oversized magical or cursed humanoids found in traditional Wabanaki territory. Lumberjack folklore also describes Bangor, Maine, as the birthplace of the legendary giant woodsman, Paul Bunyan. His official February 12, 1834, birth certificate can be found on display at the city clerk's office there, and an impressive thirty-one-foot-tall fiberglass and metal sculpture of Bunyan stands on Main Street in front of Bangor's Bass Park.

*Gitaskog* (gee-tah-skog): A southern Abenaki and Wampanoag term for a giant lake or sea serpent. See Lake Serpents; *Weewillmekq*.

Gluskap: An important giant for the Wabanaki who destroyed many ancient monsters and made the world livable for humans. See Giants.

Godaphro: A rarely used alternative name for the sidehill gouger.

Gorby (gawh-bee): A Maine and Maritime Province name for the Canada jay or gray jay (*Perisoreus canadensis*). Found throughout the northern spruce forests, this bird can easily become accustomed to people and is known for frequenting and stealing food from camps. In lumberjack days, this fearless bird was believed to the spirit of deceased woodsmen, and those who harmed it would be cursed to suffer themselves whatever harm they inflicted on the gorby. One well-known account tells of a frustrated camp cook who grabbed a thieving gorby and plucked all its feathers. The next day the man woke up to find that all of his hair had fallen out.

Gyascutus: An alternative name for the sidehill gouger.

Headless Giant: In Maliseet lore, this is a small, silent giant who can be met on the road.

Hide-behind: You can never catch a glimpse of this deadly critter. It's so quick and sly that it always remains behind you, just out of view.

Hodag: A fearsome and strange creature mostly known from Rhineland, Wisconsin, but once said to inhabit Maine.

Ice Hornets: Fearsome critters plaguing ice fishermen, these hornets make their homes in the ice.

Indian Devil: A term often synonymous with *lunksoos*, but it is also often applied to mountain lions and bigfoot-like creatures.

Jack o' Lantern: An alternative name for a will o' the wisp.

*Jipijka'm* (chih-pitch-kawm; plural: *jipijkamak*): A horned sea or lake serpent or dragon of the Micmac. See *Weewillmekq*.

Jug Woman: An evil witch, this short, ugly shapeshifter is a frequent antagonist in Wabanaki lore. She has a habit of stealing children she finds in the forest and attempting to raise them as her own. She is sometimes also called Pitcher Woman or, in Wabanaki, *Pukjinskwes* (pook-cheen-skwass).

Kaput Bird: A sad and unfortunate creature, this lopsided bird flies in smaller and smaller circles until . . . *kaput!*, it turns itself inside out.

*Kaqtukwaq* (kakw-tuk-wakw): A Micmac name for thunder giants. See Giants.

*Kci-atosis* (kih-chee ott-hoo-suss): A Wabanaki lake or sea serpent; literally, it means giant serpent. Sometimes a horned serpent. See Lake Serpents.

Kindling Cat: A western United States name for a dingmaul, this variety differs by having call like a donkey.

*Kiwakw* (keh-wah-kwah): A Wabanaki name for the wendigo. See Wendigo.

*Kiwolatomuhsisok* (gee-wuh-lah-duh-moo-sis-uck; singular: *kiwolatomuhsis*): A race of harmless little people who live near Maliseet villages mostly in New Brunswick. See Little People.

*Kluscap*: An important giant for the Wabanaki who destroyed many ancient monsters and made the world livable for humans. See Giants; Gluskap.

*Kukwes* (kook-wess): A Micmac cannibal ogre or small hairy giant of the northern forests. Unlike the wendigo, these seem to be a race to themselves.

Lake Serpents: Any of various types of giant snakes that live in lakes in the region.

Landlocked Walrus: A somewhat dangerous freshwater walrus once found in Chesuncook Lake.

Leprechaun: This magical little person is an Irish immigrant. While generally harmless in their homeland, in the Great Lakes region they were known for terrorizing and attacking lumberjacks. See Little People.

Little People: Any of several races of small magical people (three to four feet tall) found in Maine.

*Loup Cervier* (lew-sir-vee): The French word for the Canada lynx.

*Loup Garou* (lew-gar-roo): The French name for the region's werewolves.

Lucifee: An old-time name for the Canada lynx, likely a mispronunciation of the French term *loup cervier* for this animal. Lucifee is sometimes changed further to "Lucifer." Sometimes used as a term for a fearsome critter of the lumberwoods or any deadly nocturnal cat that strikes fear with its howl. See Celofay.

*Lumpeguin* (lam-peh-gwinn; plural: *lumpeguinuwok*): A small, powerful water spirit or mermaid of the Passamquoddy and Maliseet that can also appear as a little person playing along the shore. See Mermaids.

*Lunksoos* (original: lunk-soos; modern: loonk-sew): A widely used word for the "Indian Devil," the only animal Wabanaki hunters feared. Often said to be either a mountain lion or a lynx, the name is an English corruption for the Wabanaki word for the wolverine. More properly, it should be written as *Loxsis*. *Lox* is a powerful and cruel trickster in Wabanaki myths, and the ending, *-sis*, is the diminutive. In Micmac, another term for the wolverine is *keekwajoo*, which is the origin of *carcajou*, the French word for wolverine.

Lutin (lew-tahn): A French brownie or hobgoblin of a homestead.

*Manogamasak* (mah-nawn-guh-mah-sock; singular: *manogames*): A widespread race of small, harmless but ugly river elves. Noted for making clay sculptures they leave on shorelines and for having very tall and narrow faces with large noses. In Passamaquoddy, they are known as *wonakomehsok* (wuh-nah-guh-mass-uk). See Little People.

Marsh Fires: An alternative name for a will o' the wisp.

Mermaids: An aquatic race of people who are human from the waist up and fish-like from the waist down.

*Mikumwesuk* (mee-kum-wess-uk; singular: *mikumwes*): A Wabanaki race of forest elves. See Little People.

Mountain Lion: A popular name for the eastern cougar (*Puma concolor*), a large wild cat that was once found across North America but, despite persistent sightings, is officially listed as extinct in the Northeast.

*Nagumwasuk* (nah-gum-wah-suck): A race of ugly and mostly harmless river elves who live near Passamaquoddy villages. Sometimes said to be the same as the more widespread *manogamasak*. See Little People.

*Nodumkanwet* (no-dum-kan-wet): A large species of malevolent Wabanaki mermaids found on the Maine coast and large rivers. Perhaps the same as the *apodumken* of Passamaquoddy Bay. See Mermaids.

Pamola (buh-moh-lah): A dangerous winged Wabanaki creature who lives on top of Katahdin.

Panther: An alternative name for the mountain lion.

Peltin Thumper: A central Maine name for the dingmaul.

Philly Lou Bird: A fearsome bird critter that only flies backward and builds its nest upside down. See Will o' the Wisp.

Pitcher Woman: An evil witch in Wabanaki lore. This short, ugly shape-shifter is a frequent antagonist in Wabanaki stories. She has a habit of stealing children she finds or lures into the forest and attempting to raise them as her own. She is sometimes also called Jug Woman or, in Wabanaki, *Pukjinskwes* (pook-cheen-skwass).

Plunkus: An alternative name for the dingmaul.

*Pukjinskwes* (pook-cheen-skwass): A Wabanaki name for Pitcher Woman or Jug Woman.

*Pukwudgie* (bug-wuh-jih): A race of mischievous, knee-high little people resembling gnomes. In the Northeast, they can be found mostly south of Maine in Wampanoag and Delaware territory and south. See Little People.

Puma: An alternative name for the mountain lion.

Razor Shins: An undead Native American who haunts lumber camps. He must be paid with jug of liquor left outside every full moon, or he will chop off your nose, ears, or scalp with his sharp shin bones.

River Elves: A race of harmless but ugly little people. Noted for making clay sculptures that they leave on shorelines and having very tall and narrow faces with large noses. Their Wabanaki name is *manogamasak* (mah-nawn-guh-mah-sock; singular: *manogames*). See Little People.

*Sabawaelnu* (sah-buh-wahn-ill-noo): A race of large mermaids called halfway people found off coastal areas in the Micmac territory of Canada. See Mermaids.

Sasquatch: A name for bigfoot derived from the Sts'ailes people's word for hairy wildmen called "*sasq'ets.*" The Sts'ailes are a Native American group from British Columbia, Canada.

Sea Serpent: A large, undulating snake-like creature seen frequently off the coast of New England.

Sidehill Gouger: A creature of the hillsides, the left and right legs of a gouger are uneven, so they can walk around a hill and keep their back level. They are responsible for "gouging" out deep paths on mountainsides.

Silent Elves: A race of harmless little people who live near Maliseet villages mostly in New Brunswick, Canada. In Wabanaki, they are called *kiwolatomuhsisok* (gee-wuh-lah-duh-moo-sis-uck; singular: *kiwolatomuhsis*).

*Skadegamutc* (skuh-deh-guh-mooch): The spirit of a dead witch that hunts people and appears as a glowing ball of light. This Wabanaki spirit is associated with the will o' the wisp.

Slide-rock bolter: A large fearsome creature known from the western United States that hangs from steep cliff sides and slides down to devour unsuspecting people and cause rockslides. Likely related to Maine's more harmless and slow-moving wedge-ledge chomper.

Snipe: The quarry of the classic snipe-hunt prank, this animal is widely thought to be imaginary. It is actually a small brown shore bird.

Snow Snake: A fearsome snow-dwelling snake responsible for frostbite and other winter troubles. It's also the name of a Wabanaki stick game.

Snydae: This small aquatic creature of the Kennebec is part of a circular food chain with the gazerium.

Sock Saunders: A famous and troublesome Anglo-Saxon little person who causes all sorts of accidents for lumbermen. See Little People.

Specter Moose: A giant white moose found in the North Maine Woods, which can come and go undetected.

Splinter Cat: A fearsome but dim-witted and hard-headed cat who breaks tree trunks by ramming them with its head in a misguided search for food. Mostly known in the Great Lakes region. See Dingmaul.

Spreaders: A term used for river elves (*manogamasak*) who do not like trespassers and punish them by tying them up with their limbs, mouth, eyes, fingers, and toes spread apart. See Little People.

Stiff-legged Bear: In Wabanaki myth, this was a giant man-eating monster that was destroyed by Gluskap. The Wabanaki term for this creature is *Kchi Awas* (gih-chee ah-wahss), which means "giant bear." Some people believe that this may be a reference to extinct mammoths or mastodons.

Stone Dwarves: Three-foot-tall magical people who inhabit stones and mountains. The Micmac name for them is *wiklatmu'j* (wick-uh-lah-tuh-mooch). See Little People.

Stone Giants: Wabanaki giants who live in mountains. The most well known is Katahdin. See Giants.

Swamp Woman: A Wabanaki spirit woman who lives deep in cedar swamps. Clad only in moss, her moaning and wailing lures men and children into wet, lonely stretches of forest, never to be seen again. Her Wabanaki name is *Pskegdemus* (puh-skeg-day-moose).

*Tci'pilakw* (chee-buh-lock-w; alternate spellings: *geebellowk* or *chebelaque*): A dangerous spirit of the night air of the Wabanaki. It appears as a large-eyed bird creature. See Pamola.

Thunderbirds: While this creature is important in many native cultures across North America, it is absent in Wabanaki mythology. However, it shares many similarities with the thunder giants and some with *Wuchosen* (the wind bird) and *Culloo* (the bird monster). Some petroglyphs in Maine exhibit traditional thunderbird symbology. See Giants.

Thunder Giants: In Wabanaki stories, there are seven giant brothers who live in the sky and can put on bird wings and throw lightning when they battle. The southern Wabanaki term for them is *badogiak* (peh-dah-gee-yick).

Toad Woman: An alternative name for one of two Wabanaki female spirits, Swamp Woman or Jug Woman.

Tote Road Shagamaw: A scruffy and hard-to-track critter that sneaks into camp and makes off with your belongings.

Tree Squeak: A small, fearsome critter that is rarely seen but often heard squeaking in the tops of trees.

Turner Beast: Since the early 1990s, residents across central Maine in Androscroggin and Kennebec Counties have reported a large dark-colored canine beast with large or glowing eyes attacking domestic animals and frightening people.

Walrus: See Landlocked Walrus.

Wamfahoofus: A muck-dwelling one-armed creature responsible for lost footwear. Also a Vermont name for a sidehill gouger.

Wedge-ledge Chomper: A hippopotamus-sized creature responsible for carving out stone steps and causing rockslides. They have perfect camouflage as boulders.

*Weewillmekq* (wee-will-uh-meck-w): A powerful shape-shifting Wabanaki water monster, often described as a slug-like giant creature with retractable horns.

Wendigo: These wild and evil cannibal giants have hearts of ice. In most stories, they are not a specific race, but rather humans transformed by magic or a curse.

Werewolf: A terrifying cursed human or a sorcerer who can take the form of a human-wolf hybrid. See *Loup Garou.*

Wessie: A ten-foot-long snake, likely a released pet, seen by multiple witnesses in Westbrook, Maine, along the Presumpscot River in the summer of 2016. The animal likely froze to death in the winter.

Whazzit: An old New England name for a hairy wildman, bigfoot, or other ape-like creature.

*Wiklatmu'j* (wick-uh-lah-tuh-mooch): These Micmac stone dwarves are powerful but generally benign little people who live in stone or mountains. Sometimes called *pukulatmuj*. See Little People.

Wildman: An old term referring to hairy human-like creatures who may be references to bigfoot.

Will-am-alone: This strange critter is a quick little animal who drops hallucinogenic lichen balls into the eyes and ears of sleeping lumberjacks.

Will o' the Wisp: A floating light that appears in swamps and marshes and leads people astray. Wabanaki terms for related phenomena include *gas'top*, *skadegamutc* (ghost witch), and *eskuda'hit* (a fire creature).

*Wuchowsen* (wuh-chow-sun): A giant immortal bird in Wabanaki lore whose flapping wings create the winds. Sometimes called the "wind bird."

# REFERENCES


Alger, A. L. 1897. *In Indian Tents*. Boston: Roberts.

Allen, Glover M. 1930. "The Walrus in New England." *Journal of Mammalogy* 11:2, 139–45. jstor.org/stable/1374062.

American Folklore Society, eds. 1889. "Superstitions of the Passamaquoddies." *Journal of American Folklore* 2:6, 229–31. jstor.org/stable/534156.

American Folklore Society, eds. 1892. "Lutins in the Province of Quebec." *Journal of American Folklore* 5:19, 327–28. jstor.org/stable/533243.

Baron, D. 2011. "The Cougar Behind Your Trash Can." *New York Times*, July 27, p. A27. Retrieved from nytimes.com/2011/07/29/opinion/the-cougar-behind-your-trash-can.html.

Beaudoin, R. 1968. Student paper on French-Canadian folklore. Northeast Archives of Folklore and Oral History, na455.

Beck, H. P. 1957. *The Folklore of Maine.* Philadelphia: J.B. Lippincott Co.

Bigfootencounters. 2018. State by State Listings: Maine. bigfootencounters.com/sbs/me.html.

Botkin, B. A. 1947. *A Treasury of New England Folklore.* Revised edition. New York: Bonanza Books.

Briggs, K. M. 1976. "Little People of the Passamaquoddy Indians." In *An Encyclopedia of Fairies*, 268–70. New York: Pantheon Books.

Bruchac, J. 1998. *The Waters Between: A Novel of the Dawn Land.* Hanover, NH: University Press of New England.

Bruchac, J. 2009. *Night Wings*. New York: HarperCollins.

Bruchac, J., & J. Bruchac. 1998. *When the Chenoo Howls: Native American Tales of Terror*. New York: Walker and Company.

Brynn, C. 2017. "Lake Willoughby: Legend of the Lake Monster." *Brynn Swim: Never Give Up*. brynnswim.com/lake-willoughby-legend-of-the-lake-monster/.

Burmon, A. 2012. "Lake Memphremagog: The Legend of Memphre, a Monster Which Sits in the Quebec/Vermont Lake." *Huffington Post: Travel*. huffingtonpost.com/2012/10/15/quebecs-lake-memphremagog_n_1966470.html.

Carr, J. W., & G. D. Chase. 1912. "A Word-List from Eastern Maine." *Dialect Notes: Volume III (Parts I–VIII, 1905–1912)*, pp. 239–51. Reprinted by the University of Alabama.

*Centennial Celebration, and Dedication of Town Hall, Orono, Maine, March 3, 1874*. Portland: Bailey & Noyes. archive.org/details/centennialcelebr00unse.

*Chicago Daily Tribune* Editors. 1887. "The Monster of Skiff Lake." *Chicago Daily Tribune*, August 7, p. 15.

Coleman, L. 2007. "Maine's Mystery Moose." *Cryptomundo: For Bigfoot, Lake Monsters, Sea Serpents and More*, February 17. cryptomundo.com/cryptozoo-news/myst-moose/.

Coleman, L. 2013. *Monsters of Massachusetts*. Mechanicsburg, PA: Stackpole Books.

Coleman, L., & P. Huyghe. 2003. *The Field Guide to Lake Monsters, Sea Serpents and Other Mystery Denizens of the the Deep*. New York: Jeremy P. Tarcher/Penguin.

Cormier, G. 1965. Student paper on devils, lutin, etc. Northeast Archives of Folklore and Oral History, na81.

Cox, W. T. 1910. *Fearsome Creatures of the Lumberwoods*. Washington, DC: Judd & Detweiler, Inc. fearsomecreaturesofthelumberwoods.com/home.htm.

Dell'Amore, C. 2015. "What's a Ghost Moose? How Ticks Are Killing an Iconic Animal." *National Geographic*, June 1. news.nationalgeographic.com/2015/06/150601-ghost-moose-animals-science-new-england-environment/.

Downing, R. L. 1984. "The Search for Cougars in the Eastern United States." *Cryptozoology* 3, pp. 31–49. easterncougar.org/pdfs/Robert_Downing.pdf.

Dudley, J. 2010. "Indian Devils." *Alexander-Crawford Historical Society Newsletter* (Alexander, Maine). mainething.com/alexander/memories/INDIAN%20DEVILS.htm.

Dudley, J. 2010. "Pocomoonshine Lake Monster." *Alexander-Crawford Historical Society Newsletter* (Alexander, Maine). mainething.com/alexander/memories/POCOMOONSHINE%20LAKE%20MONSTER.htm.

Dudley, J. 2011. "Tree Squeak." *Alexander-Crawford Historical Society Newsletter* (Alexander, Maine). mainething.com/alexander/INTERVIEWS/TREE%20SQUEAK.htm.

Dudley, M. 1965. Student paper on horror stories, place names, etc. Northeast Archives of Folklore and Oral History, na105.

Eckstorm, F. H. N.d. FANNIE HARDY ECKSTORM PAPERS 1865–1946—RE: Little People. Box 6, folder 20: "Legends of the Passamaquodies," Box 6, folder 52: "The Indian Fairies," Box 4, folder 50: "Indian Fairies." Special Collections, Raymond H. Fogler Library, University of Maine.

Eckstorm, F. H. N.d. FANNIE HARDY ECKSTORM PAPERS 1865–1946—RE: Mermen. Box 6, folder 65: "Mermen and Underwater People." Special Collections, Raymond H. Fogler Library, University of Maine.

Eckstorm, F. H. N.d. FANNIE HARDY ECKSTORM PAPERS 1865–1946—RE: Keewahquee. Box 6, folder 25: "The Bone-Breaker," Box 6, folder 34: "Clara Neptune, May 28, 1917. A Kewahqee Story." Special Collections, Raymond H. Fogler Library, University of Maine.

Eckstorm, F. H. 1924. "The Katahdin Legends." *Appalachian Mountain Club*, n.s., XVI, 39–52.

Eckstorm, F. H. 1936. FANNIE HARDY ECKSTORM PAPERS 1865–1946. Box 6, folder 11: "Natural History Comparative List of

Animals Birds, Fishes, Insects." Special Collections, Raymond H. Fogler Library, University of Maine.
Eckstorm, F. H. 1945. *Old John Neptune and Other Maine Indian Shamans.* Portland, ME: Southworth-Anthoensen Press.
Edgar, M. 1940. "Imaginary Animals of Northern Minnesota." *Minnesota History* 21:4 (December), 353–56.
Etravelmaine.com. N.d. "Maine Sea Serpents and Lake Monsters" & "Bigfoot Sightings in Maine." In Attractions: Strange Maine. etravel maine.com/attractions/strange-maine/.
Farrell, J. C. 1965. Student paper on witch stories, other stories. Northeast Archives of Folklore and Oral History, na138.
Fewkes, J. W. 1890. "A Contribution to Passamaquoddy Folk-Lore." *Journal of American Folklore* III, pp. 257–80.
Fraser, M. L. N.d. Folklore of Nova Scotia. Self-published. archive.org/ details/folkloreofnovasc00frasuoft/page/n5.
Gray, T. M. 2010. *New England Graveside Tales.* Atglen, PA: Schiffer.
Hall, C., & Thomas, J. 1991. *Chimney Pond Tales: Yarns Told by Leroy Dudley.* Cumberland Center, ME: Pomola Press.
Hardy, Fannie P. 1891. "The Sportsman Tourist: In the Region Round Nicatowis." *Forest and Stream* 36: 3rd ed. Charles Hallock, William A. Bruette, pp. 42–43.
Haviland, W. A., & M. W. Power. 1981. *The Original Vermonters: Native Inhabitants, Past and Present.* Hanover, NH: University Press of New England.
Hay, T. H. 1971. "The Windigo Psychosis: Psychodynamic, Cultural, and Social. Factors in Aberrant Behavior." *American Anthropologist,* Issue 73, pp. 1–19. anthrosource.onlinelibrary.wiley.com/doi/pdf/10.1525/ aa.1971.73.1.02a00010.
Hobbs, C. W. 1886. *Lynn and Surroundings.* Lynn, MA: Lewis and Winship. archive.org/details/lynnsurroundings00inhobb/.
Iceshanty Community. 2007. "Snow Snakes": forum topic post in IceShanty.com's Ice Fishing Community » Maine » Ice Fishing Maine. Post 59754. Reply 34-35 about ice hornets. Original thread

date: November 7, 2007, 04:26 p.m. iceshanty.com/ice_fishing/index.php?topic=59754.

Ives, E. D., ed. 1998. "The Little People" & "Lost Hunters I." In *Northeast Folklore Volume VI: 1964—Malecite and Passamaquoddy Tales*, 2nd ed. Maine Folklife Center. University of Maine, Orono, Maine. umaine.edu/folklife/publications/northeast-folklore-2/miscellaneous-malecite-tales/.

Jesuits & R. G. Thwaites. 1899. "Chapter III. Letter Written to Reverend Father Hie-Rosme Lallemant, Superior of the Missions of the Society of Jesus in New France, 1661." *The Jesuit Relations and Allied Documents: Travels and Explorations of the Jesuit Missionaries in New France, 1610–1791, Volume 46*, 251–81. Cleveland, OH: Burrows Brothers Co. archive.org/details/jesuits46jesuuoft.

Josselyn, J. 1865. *An Account of Two Voyages to New England, Made during the Years 1638, 1663.* Boston: William Veazie. archive.org/details/accountoftwovoya00joss/page/22.

Julian, M. R., & V. Toney. 1999. "Wiklatmu'j: The Little Person." Centre for Excellence: Mi'kmaw Kina'matnewey, Membertou, Nova Scotia. firstnationhelp.com/ali/wiklatmuj/.

Krohn, W. B. 2005. "Manly Hardy (1832–1910): The Life and Writing of a Maine Fur-Buyer, Hunter, and Naturalist." *Northeast Folklore* XXXVIII (Maine Folklife Center, Orono, ME).

Krohn, W. B., & C. L. Hoving. 2010. *Early Maine Wildlife: Historical Accounts of Canada Lynx, Moose, Mountain Lion, White-tailed Deer, Wolverine, Wolves, and Woodland Caribou, 1603–1930.* Orono: University of Maine Press.

Leland, C. G. 1884. *The Algonquin Legends of New England.* London: Sampson Low.

Leland, C. G., & J. D. Prince. 1902. *Kulóskap the Master: And Other Algonkin Poems.* New York: Funk & Wagnalls.

Lenik, E. J. 2010. "Mythic Creatures: Serpents, Dragons, & Sea Monsters in Northeastern Rock Art." *Archaeology of Eastern North America* 38, pp. 17–37. jstor.org/stable/40914539.

Macdonald, D. 1987. "Walrus." In *The Encyclopedia of Mammals*, 264–69. New York: Facts on File Publications.

McCollough, M., et al. 2003. *Maine's Endangered and Threatened Wildlife.* Augusta: Maine Department of Inland Fisheries and Wildlife.

Mead, A., & A. Neptune. 1996. *Giants of the Dawnland: Ancient Wabanaki Tales.* Cumberland Center, ME: Loose Cannon Press.

Moores, J. E. 2015. *Snotgrass*. Self-published, jemoores.com.

North Atlantic Region National Park Service, 1994. *Acadian Culture in Maine: Oral Traditions*: Web Edition Reprint by University of Maine at Fort Kent. acim.umfk.maine.edu/oral_traditions.html.

O'Neill, J. P. 1999. *The Great New England Sea Serpent.* Camden, ME: Down East Books.

Packard, Dwight A. 2016, July. Personal communications regarding wedge-ledge chompers, freshwater tree squeaks, peltin thumpers, side-hill gougers, and youmissedits.

Packard, Gerald. 2016, August. Personal communication regarding kaput birds.

Packard, M. 1974. *A History of Packard's Camps 1894–1916, Sebec Lake, Maine*. Self-published by Mary P. Rankin.

Packard, Marlborough. 2016, July. Personal communication regarding peltin thumpers.

Parent, M., & J. Olivier. 1996. "The Lutin and the Hay Wagon." *Of Kings and Fools*. Little Rock, AR: August House.

Paul, G. E. 2004. "Tales from the Mi'kmaq Nation's Precious Folklore: Wiklatmu'j—Stone People." *We Were Not the Savages: First Nation History.* Edited by D. N. Paul. http://danielnpaul.com/Mi%27kmaq Culture.html.

Paul, P. N.d. "Geow-lud-mo-sis-eg." *Little People: A Native American Lore.* Retrieved January 4, 2015, from ilhawaii.net/~stony/lore10.html.

Perham, J. 2010. "The Loup Garou." *Tales from the Maine Woods, Vol. I.* Smasheasy, Joe Perham's Maine Humor.

Perham, J. 2010. "Mark, Mark." *Tales from the Maine Woods, Vol. II.* Smasheasy, Joe Perham's Maine Humor.

Powell, H., ed. 2017. "Wilson's Snipe." *All about Birds.* Cornell Lab of Ornithology. allaboutbirds.org/guide/Wilsons_Snipe/overview.

Prince, J. D. 1921. *Passamaquoddy Texts: Vol. X.* American Ethnological Society. New York: G.E. Schert & Co. archive.org/details/passamaquoddyte00pringoog.

Putnam, W. L. 1986. *Joe Dodge.* Flagstaff, AZ: Light Technology Publishing.

Rand, S. T. 1894. *Legends of the Micmacs.* New York: Longman, Grey, and Co. archive.org/details/cihm_12305.

Ricker, N. 2013. "Bigfoot in Maine? 10-Foot-Tall 'Wild Man' Was Killed in 1886, Newspapers Reported." *Bangor Daily News*, October 27. bangordailynews.com/2013/10/27/news/state/bigfoot-in-maine-10-foot-tall-wild-man-was-killed-in-1886-newspapers-reported/.

Robinson, R. E. 1894. *Danvis Folks.* Boston: Houghton Mifflin. archive.org/details/danvisfolks00robiuoft/page/n6.

Rolde, N., & WCBB. 1984. *So You Think You Know Maine.* Gardiner, ME: Harpswell Press.

Sacramento Union. 1911. "'Specter Moose' Seen Once More." *Sacramento Union*, no. 26 (November). California Digital Newspaper Collection. cdnc.ucr.edu/cgi-bin/cdnc?a=d&d=SU19111126.2.16.

Schmidtt, C. 2010. "Maine's First Lake." *Friends of Acadia Journal* (Spring), 10–11.

Skinner, C. M. 1896. "Storied Waters, Cliffs, and Mountains." In *American Myths and Legends, Vol. 2*, 10th edition, 299. Philadelphia: J.B. Lippincott Co. archive.org/details/mythslegendsofou02skin.

Skinner, C. M. 1903. "Maine Woodland Terrors." In *American Myths and Legends, Vol. 1*, 33–40. Philadelphia: J.B. Lippincott Co. archive.org/details/americanmythsleg01skin.

Souliere, M. Y. 2010. *Strange Maine: True Tales from the Pine Tree State.* Charleston, SC: History Press.

Speck, F. G. 1919. "Penobscot Shamanism." *Memoirs of the American Anthropological Association* VI:4, 237–88.

Speck, F. G. 1926. "Wawenock Myth Texts from Maine." *ARBAE* XLIII, 165–97.

Speck, F. G. 1935. "Penobscot Tales and Religious Beliefs." *Journal of American Folklore* 48:187, 1–107. jstore.org/stable/535328.

Speck, F. G. 1940. *Penobscot Man*. Philadelphia: University of Pennsylvania Press.

Spray, Carole. 1979. *Will o' the Wisp: Folk Tales and Legends of New Brunswick*. Fredericton, New Brunswick: Brunswick Press.

Springer, J. S. 1851. *Forest Life and Forest Trees: Comprising Winter Camp-Life among the Loggers, and Wild-Wood Adventures*. New York: Harper & Brothers.

Stamp, Harley. 1915. "The Water-Fairies." *Journal of American Folklore* 28:109, 310–16. jstor.org/stable/534430.

Thoreau, H. D. 1864. *The Maine Woods*. Boston, MA: Ticknor & Fields. archive.org/details/mainewoods00thorrich.

Tryon, H. H. 1939. *Fearsome Critters*. Cornwall, NY: Idlewild Press. lumberwoods.com/heading.htm.

U.S. Fish and Wildlife Service. 2011. "Eastern Cougar: Questions and Answers about the Five-Year Review." Northeast Region U.S. Fish and Wildlife Service. fws.gov/northeast/ecougar/QA.html.

U.S. Fish and Wildlife Service. 2015. "Eastern Cougar: *Felis concolor couguar*." Northeast Region U.S. Fish and Wildlife Service. fws.gov/northeast/ecougar/pdf/Easterncougar2015.pdf.

U.S. Fish and Wildlife Service. 2018. "Long Extinct Eastern Cougar to Be Removed from Endangered Species List Correcting Lingering Anomaly." News Bulletin, January 22, 2018. fws.gov/northeast/ecougar/pdf/Cougar_News_Bulletin_Final_1_18.pdf.

Vetromile, E. 1866. *The Abnakis and Their History*. New York: J.B. Kirker. archive.org/details/abnakistheirhist00vetr/.

Violette, C. 1968. Student paper on recipe and French-Canadian stories. Northeast Archives of Folklore and Oral History, na475.

Wallis, W. D., & R. S. Wallis. 1955. *The Micmac Indians of Eastern Canada*. Minneapolis: University of Minnesota Press.

Wallis, W. D., & R. S. Wallis. 1957. "The Malecite Indians of New Brunswick." *National Museum of Canada, Bulletin*, No. 148.

Wampus Society. N.d. *Fearsome Creatures of the Northwoods: A Dictionary of North American Tall Tale Creatures*. lumberwoods.com/dictionary.htm.

Whitehead, R. H. 1988. *Stories from the Six Worlds: Micmac Legends*. Halifax, Nova Scotia: Nimbus Publishing Limited.

Williamson, W. D. 1832. *The History of the State of Maine; From Its First Discovery, A. D. 1602, to the Separation, A. D. 1820, Inclusive*. Vol. I. Hallowell, ME: Glazier Masters & Co. archive.org/details/historyofstateof01will_0/page/n3.

Wiseman, F. M., & ELNU Abenaki Tribe. 2006. "*Tsoheac*, the Wabenaki Snow Snake Game." ELNU Abenaki Tribe. elnuabenakitribe.org/SnowSnakes.html.

Wyman, Walker D. 1978. *Mythical Creatures of the USA and Canada*. River Falls: University of Wisconsin–River Falls Press.

## IMAGE CREDITS

All illustrations by Dan Kirchoff, except:

- Bigfoot Tracks: Illustration by Christopher Packard.
- Brownie: Illustration by Alice B. Woodward, from J. Ewing (1920), *The Brownies and Other Tales.*
- Burton Marlborough Packard: Packard family picture, ca. 1920. Courtesy of Gerald Packard.
- *Chenoo/Mikumwes*: Illustration by Tomah Josephs, from C. G. Leland (1884), *The Algonquin Legends of New England.*
- Christopher Packard: Photograph by Justin Levesque.
- Clay Concretion Fairy Stones: Photograph by Christopher Packard.
- Lake Serpent Petroglyphs: Photograph by Christopher Packard.
- Mermaid Map: H. Scherer (1702), *Idea naturalis Americae Borealis digito dei formata geographice proposita an MDCC* (Glen McLaughlin Map Collection of California as an Island, Stanford Libraries).
- Mountain Lion Tracks: Illustration by Christopher Packard.
- Pamola: Baxter Brewing Logo: Used with permission of Baxter Brewing Company.

- Pamola as a Giant: Unnamed illustrator in E. Vetromile (1866), *The Abnakis and Their History*.
- Pamola Signature Mark: Chief Arexes for the *Centennial Celebration and Dedication of Town Hall, Orono, Maine, March 3, 1874* (Portland: Bailey & Noyes).
- Sea Serpent: Unnamed illustrator in C. W. Hobbs (1886), *Lynn and Surroundings*.
- Snow Snakes: Unnamed illustrator in W. H. Holmes (1895), *Annual Report of the Bureau of American Ethnology to the Secretary of the Smithsonian Institution* (Washington, DC: U.S. Government Printing Office).
- Will o' the Wisp: Illustration by Arthur Rackham (1908).
- Wolf: Photograph by Gary Kramer, U.S. Fish and Wildlife Service, National Conservation Training Center Image Library.

# ABOUT THE AUTHOR

**CHRISTOPHER PACKARD** is a full-time high school science teacher and also a trail runner, swordfighter, storyteller, and outdoor adventurer. When not teaching, writing, or wandering in the wilds, he can often be found on his small homestead in Hampden, Maine, gardening, raising chickens, and spending time with his wife and sons. He has earned some pieces of paper that say things about degrees in biology and education. But most of his learning has come from his passion for discovery and his drive to bring people together and connect to the place where they live. Christopher has many years of experience teaching about natural history and science at nature centers, summer camps, museums, colleges, and secondary school classrooms.

Christopher's family has been building ships, lumbering, hunting, trapping, guiding, telling tales, and running wilderness resort hotels in Maine since before the Civil War. He continues this family tradition by being handy with a chainsaw, a shotgun, and a map. Among many other adventures, he has climbed Katahdin, hiked the 100 Mile Wilderness, paddled the Allagash Wilderness Waterway, and run across Waldo County on the Hills to Sea Trail in a single day. Christopher was born and raised in Ohio, spending summers in Maine until finally making it his full-time home in 2007.